SUNRUINED

Seven bleak stories by
Andersen Prunty

GRINDHOUSE PRESS

Published by Grindhouse Press
POB 292644
Dayton, OH 45429
www.grindhousepress.com

Sunruined: Horror Stories
Grindhouse Press #009
ISBN-13: 978-0-9849692-2-7
ISBN-10: 0984969225
Copyright © 2012 by Andersen Prunty. All rights reserved.

This book is a work of fiction.

Cover design copyright © 2012 by Matthew Revert
www.matthewrevert.com

Grindhouse Press logo copyright © 2012 by Brandon Duncan
www.corporatedemon.com

Cover photograph © 2012 by Michel Omar Berrospé

Also by Andersen Prunty

The Driver's Guide to Hitting Pedestrians

Hi I'm a Social Disease: Horror Stories

Fuckness

The Sorrow King

Slag Attack

My Fake War

Morning is Dead

The Beard

Zerostrata

Jack and Mr. Grin

The Overwhelming Urge

Sunruined

Contents

The Jackthief
1

The Screaming Orchard
7

Glowers Point
25

Cruel Women with Whiplike Smiles
45

The Smoke of Samuel
55

Sad Clown, Kentucky
71

Sunruined
85

The Jackthief

Oletta Goom woke up on the morning of October 31st and went into the baby's room, knowing exactly what she would find.

Emptiness.

The crib stood in the middle of the room, white cotton blankets piled up against one side. Outside, the wind, turned cold with the season, spat at the house and invaded the open window. Oletta grabbed the worn wooden rail of the crib with a bony hand and cried, her tears running down her wrinkled face and falling onto the cotton sheet that still smelled faintly of Jacquelyn. "Jack," Oletta had called her.

But now Jack was gone.

Just like all of the girls that had come before her. And it was always on this day, the first birthday, Halloween, that the Jackthief came and took them away. Now she would have to wait another year before going into the haunted woods to claim her prize.

Unless she could find out where the Jackthief took the babies. Unless she could get this one back.

Oletta had been several years younger when she had retreated to her house in the woods. Perhaps it was more of a shack, but it served the purposes of shelter and warmth just fine and that was all she needed now. Shelter and warmth. Maybe it wasn't all she *wanted*, but it was all she needed, along with a little food every now and then.

What Oletta wanted more than anything was a baby. She was not a young woman anymore, twenty years past childbearing age, but that desire had never left her. It was only since the death of her husband that she realized it was an impossibility. Before, she had always prayed for a miracle. Maybe, she had thought, God would fix whatever was broken inside of her and she would finally get pregnant. But it was never meant to be.

So her husband had died and she had moved to the woods feeling like, if she was going to be alone, she was going to do it right.

But moving to the woods proved to be the source of more joy and sorrow than she would ever know.

It was there she met the Jackthief. There, during the strangest of circumstances.

Summer was buried, Halloween standing atop it like a cold gray tombstone, and Oletta didn't see how she was going to spend a winter alone in the tiny shack. She figured her best days were well behind her and there weren't going to be any good ones ahead. She found a length of strong rope in the old woodshed. She was going to take the rope out into the woods, find a good sturdy branch, and hang herself. She didn't plan on learning how to do it proper. If she had to dangle for a while, choking on her own windpipe, then she just figured that would be penance for the awesome sin she was about to undertake.

After a brief survey, she found a branch that would do the trick. The rope was slung around her neck to give her frail arms the strength to carry an old wooden ladder. It was a gray day. The clouds were bloated black-gray, threatening rain. Maybe, if it rained, it would help weigh down her body.

It took about a half an hour to make sure everything was in

place. She figured the knot was strong enough to do the trick. Climbing to the top of the ladder, the fiber of the rope scratchy around her neck, the sky rumbled a hungry growl and she hoped it would drown out the sound of her strangling to death.

Standing at the top of the ladder, she wondered if she was doing the right thing. But this wasn't a spontaneous decision. It was something she had thought about for a very long time. This was the only way out. The lonely days had become unendurable and she was too proud to be stuck in this constant state of self-pity.

The sky screamed.

Oletta took a deep breath and kicked the ladder away.

She dropped. The rope tightened around her neck.

And then broke.

She fell to the ground, lightning streaked across the sky, fat cold drops of rain hammered down, and her life changed forever.

On the other side of the tree she had tried to use to kill herself, she heard a baby crying. Oletta unfastened the rope from around her neck, not believing what it was she thought she heard. Nursing a twisted ankle, she trudged through the dead leaves, turned soggy, until she found the source of the crying.

When she saw the baby, swaddled in black cloth, at the base of the tree, her face split and her tears mingled with the beating rain. Stooping down, she picked up the baby and took it back to the house, wanting to get it out of the rain, wanting to get it into the warmth.

Sometimes, Oletta knew, when a person wanted something so much, it was not necessary to question the source. It was not necessary to question the truth or validity behind that desire. A Christian wanted a God to save her and an afterlife to house her soul when she dies. The Christian does not question these things, she believes them and calls that belief faith. So Oletta believed in her new baby maybe not so much as born but given to her on this Halloween day.

She took it home with her. First she named her Jacquelyn and called her Jack. She loved Jack. She fed her and sang to her and talked to her and cared for her and took her everywhere she went. She even took her into the town to buy food and clothes, not caring if the folk talked and wondered. They would, Oletta knew, come up with their own reasons why she now had a baby and those reasons could not come even remotely close to the fantastic truth.

For exactly one year, Oletta was the mother of a beautiful baby.

On Jack's first birthday, Oletta opened the door to her room and discovered the baby gone, the bedroom window open, a cold wind blowing in. The following year, she searched for baby Jack. Searched and mourned because she knew the baby was gone.

That was the worst year of Oletta's life, having had something and then lost it. Each day was worse than the one before. Her life had become a spiraling black nightmare as she wondered about who would steal the only thing she had ever wanted. She never found the Jackthief but she had a picture of him in her mind.

The Jackthief was carved from wood and bone. He traveled by moonlight and drank the sorrow of others. He was drawn to this sorrow and, drunk off it, had to create more. Oletta knew the Jackthief had always been there. He was the one who had snapped the rope when the only thing she wanted to do was snap her neck. He did it because she had not suffered enough. She was a well of suffering and the Jackthief had not drunk the last of that well. So he had let her love the baby for a year. And just as quickly, he had taken it away. Now he surrounded her in the woods, watching her, mocking her silently as she searched and searched.

A year later, she found baby Jack in the same place she had found her two years earlier. The baby was the same size as the very first time Oletta found her and she had a distinct feeling of falling back two years in time. But, once again, the sorrow had lifted. She had her baby. Maybe the circumstances were not normal. Maybe they weren't even believable, but it was nice to hold Jack in her arms once again and feel a year of sadness melt away.

Over the next two years, the cycle repeated itself.

Always from Halloween to Halloween. One year of joy. One of sorrow. One a trick. The other, of course, a treat.

After losing Jack again, Oletta did not search for her.

She sat in her house and waited, her mind expanding out into that depressed madness, knowing her time would come again. Yet knowing that did not make it easier. The only thing she could think of was the year after that, when she would have to go without the baby again. The Trickyear. And, after all, wasn't the point of having a baby to watch it grow? To shape it and give it a good life? To see what kind of adult it became?

That year, Oletta decided she was not going to go without Jack again.

On October 31st, when she found Jack under the tree, Oletta said to her, "I'm never letting you go. If he takes you again, I will find you." And she took the baby back home and they had another good year—the Treatyear—but now the time had come again and Oletta stood in an empty room, surrounded by nightmares.

That morning, she left the house in search of the Jackthief, knowing he was out there, somewhere. She was not going to go back home until she found the baby. For days, she wandered deeper into the woods, the noose of cold and hunger wrapping around her neck.

Madness rats nibbled at her brain. She followed the Jackthief. She followed his scent. He smelled like wax and fallen leaves. He smelled like memories. Some nights, she thought she heard the baby crying. Some nights, she thought she heard the Jackthief laughing.

She became hungry and confused, knowing she was too far from her house to ever get back. The sorrow was black and swollen in her mind. She let it grow, knowing that the greater the sorrow, the more likely she was to see the Jackthief. And then she could take her baby back.

On the night of her death, before the Jackthief came and took the sorrow away for good, Oletta couldn't open her eyes. She couldn't see the Jackthief. But she thought she could open her eyes far enough to see the little black bundle he held in his arms. She pawed at the blankets, wanting to touch Jack's soft baby skin one last time but the thing inside the blankets was not Jack.

It was carved from wood and bone.

It smelled like burning wax and dead leaves.

And when it opened its mouth, it didn't want milk, it wanted to drink sorrow and a whole life filled with longing. And when it satiated itself on those things, it laughed, and moved onto the next person in the next town.

The Screaming Orchard

"You know, we could just walk," Nie said. Her real name was Stephanie, but she hated that name and all of its usual derivatives.

Chris, lying on top of the ancient baby blue Escort said, "I'm way too high to walk. Probably fall down."

"That was your idea."

"Maybe somebody'll come along and pick us up."

"Look around you, Chris. This road probably sees like two cars a day and we're one of them. Besides, you have blood all over you."

"And that, sweetie, was *your* idea."

"I thought it would be fun to get out of the house. There *are* other things to do besides messing around in your parents' basement, you know."

"Maybe for you. You're all *I* need. Besides, I promised them I'd stay and pass out candy."

"You left the bowl out, didn't you?"

"Yeah. But you know how that is. One of those punks'll come along and take all the candy, probably the bowl with it, and then some other punks will egg the house or something because they think we're *those people* who are too cheap to give out candy."

"Christ, you think too much."

"I *think* we should have stayed there."

Nie looked around them, the endless fields of golden brown corn divided only by the narrow strip of the gray road. *At least it's warm*, she told herself. A perfect day to go trick-or-treating, if she were like four years younger. She had been looking forward to going to Donna's party and Chris's indifference was really starting to irritate her.

"What the fuck are you supposed to *be*, anyway?" she asked him.

"I'm a butcher," he said, staring up at the clear blue sky.

"And that's scary how?"

"I don't know. I just thought it looked grisly." He sat up, brought his feet around the side of the car and scooted off.

"You look like a murdering soda jerk."

"Do they still have those?"

"I don't know."

"Butchers wear hats, don't they?"

"I don't know *what* butchers wear."

"And what are you supposed to be?"

"I'm a ghoul."

"I think this is just your excuse to look goth."

"Well, I don't know what a ghoul looks like."

"That's okay. You look hot. I mean it."

"Didn't you get enough last night?" She pulled her black shawl over the cleavage showing above the black corset.

"Enough of you? Never."

"But you're too high to walk?"

"Completely different muscles."

"Pervert. Besides, I couldn't possibly fuck anyone who has their hands in animal parts all day."

"Jeez, vegetarians."

"And my boyfriend's vegetarian. He wouldn't like that."

Chris walked up to her and put his hands on her hips. "Have I told you how much I like role playing?"

He leaned down to kiss her black lips and she pulled away.

"Car," she said.

Chris turned and squinted down the road.

"Van," he said. "A white, unmarked van. We should hide rather than trying to bum a ride from them."

Nie watched the van come toward them from the darkening eastern horizon.

"But," she said. "If we can get them to take us back to your house then I can call a tow truck and we can take your car to the party. I'll make it worth your while."

She reached down and cupped his stiff penis with her palm and whispered into his ear, "Don't you want to know what it feels like to fuck the dead?"

Chris smiled and said, "Okay, okay. You win."

Men are such suckers, Nie thought.

They both edged up to the side of the road and waved their hands.

The van, all white with tinted windows wrapping around the side and back, pulled to a stop just past them.

Chris ran up to the driver's side door. The tinted window rolled down and Chris struggled not to laugh at the man in front of him. The man had curly brown hair that looked like it was either a bad perm or a wig, cut in half by a white headband with a red stripe running along the middle. His face was full and round, outdated aviator sunglasses covering his eyes. A brown mustache occluded his top lip. The same exact-looking man sat in the passenger seat.

"Anything we can do for you?" the driver asked.

Chris stammered and then said, "Yeah, my girlfriend's car broke down and we were wondering if you could possibly give us a lift back into town."

"Well, we was kinda headed the other way."

"We could pay you for gas and time. Just tell me what you need." Chris thought about Nie's promise and realized how desperately he wanted to get home.

"No, that ain't necessary. We can probably just go through town and get where we was goin just the same." Then he turned to his partner. "You think?"

His partner bobbed his white man's afro in agreement.

"Great." Chris smiled broadly. "Thanks a lot, you guys."

"Yeah, no problem. Y'all can just climb in back there."

Chris walked around behind the van and jerked his head at Nie. He let her get up close to him and said, "These guys are kind of strange," before yanking back the van's sliding door.

"Hey there," the guy in the driver's seat said when he saw Nie.

"Hi. Thanks guys," she said, pulling the van door shut.

"Looks like you guys are ready for Halloween."

"Yeah," Nie said. "What are you guys supposed to be?" She asked that because she was convinced they were both wearing wigs and, once inside the van, she noticed they were also dressed the same. They wore matching, outdated track uniforms, white tanktops stretched over their doughy skin and old red running shorts that were way too short. Without seeing them, Nie could imagine the knee-high tube socks, red stripes at the top.

"Whaddya mean?" the driver asked.

"For Halloween?" Nie said.

"Oh," the driver chuckled. "We ain't dressed for Halloween. We're twins. Name's Vincent. Both of us. Our parents way of a sick joke, I guess."

"I'm Chris," Chris volunteered, since Nie was still choking on her foot. "This is my girlfriend, Nie."

"*Knee?*"

"Yeah, spelled different, but said just like those things in the middle of your legs."

The van slowly pulled away from the curb. The driver shook his head and said, "Fraid you're not right about that. We was born without knees. Turn around n show em there, Vince."

The passenger swiveled around in his seat and straightened out his legs to show them how the expansive lower thigh joined almost evenly with the calf. He rapped his knuckles on the flesh and it made a doughy patter sound.

"That bone there," he said. "For those that's got em anyway, is called the patella. That's what we was born without—the patella. I guess we still got the muscles and everything."

Chris and Nie gaped in awe.

After riding silently for a few minutes, Nie noticed they weren't going in the direction of town. She didn't think anything was strange at first because she thought maybe the twins were planning on taking one of the side roads farther up.

She looked at Chris and mouthed, "Where the hell are we going?"

To allay her suspicions, Chris asked, "So, you guys from around here?"

"Huh-uh," the driver said. "We're from over in Preston."

"Never heard of it," Chris said. "You know how to get back to town from here?"

"Now, we're not going there just yet. We got some stuff to do. Might could use your help."

"We kind of needed to get back in a hurry," Nie said, icy fingers of fear spreading through her.

"Well, now your boyfriend here, he was willin to pay us, said anything you want... I reckon we need us some help."

Nie leaned forward in her seat and said, "That's not part of the deal. If you want cash, that's fine, whatever you want, but we've got places to be and... parents that are expecting us."

"Just ease up, honey. We ain't a couple of sickies. We just need your help, that's all."

Nie clenched her jaws, ready to lash out at them. Chris reached over and put his hand on her knee and spoke in her place.

"What, exactly, will we be helping you with?"

"Just a little, uh..." the driver looked at the passenger and they both chuckled, "Horticulture."

"I don't understand," Chris said.

"You ever hear tale of the June tree?"

"No," Chris said.

"Don't rightly know why they call it the June tree, since it blooms in October."

"I've never *heard* of a tree blooming in October," Nie sneered.

"Well, this'n does. At least it's rumored to. I guess the tree must've been named June or something before."

"Before what?" Chris asked.

"The way the story goes, a number of years back, prob'ly before any of us was even born, there's this girl named June who got raped and killed out by some woods. But that ain't the really strange part. I mean, that shit happens every day. But now they say that, if you was to be standin and lookin at this old dead tree that happens to be bout round where they say the girl was murdered, and it was a full moon on Halloween, you'd see the tree become that girl. You'd see it bloom."

"That's ridiculous," Nie said.

The passenger turned around and looked at her and, for the first time, she saw that he had a red number two on his tank top. It made her think of Thing One and Thing Two, from *The Cat in the Hat*. "It's nothin to be afraid of. It's not like the tree's gonna jump out and *getcha*."

And then he shot his arms out and squeezed the inside of Nie's thighs, a little too close to her crotch for Chris's liking. But Nie took care of herself. After jumping nearly to the roof of the van, she roped out her right arm and punched the guy in the face.

The man retreated back into his seat holding his mouth and Nie was pretty sure he was sobbing. She was surprised when the van didn't stop and they weren't asked to leave.

Then she heard the passenger say, "She hit me, Vin."

The driver reached out and patted his brother's quivering shoulder. "That's all right, buddy. She didn't mean it. Did you, sweetie?"

"Yeah, I did, shitface." She wasn't looking at the driver. She was turned in her seat, scanning the back of the van, looking for some means of escape. On the floor in front of the backseat, she spotted a shovel, a bag of dirt, and a large plastic pot. She looked at Chris and motioned toward the shovel.

He reached back for it as the driver said, "You know, you kids got a funny way of showing gratitude."

Chris quickly grabbed the shovel and, with his hands somewhere around the middle, wielded it in front of him.

"Okay, guys," he said. "Stop the van. We wanna get out."

Chris met the driver's shaded eyes in the rearview mirror as the man said, "I think you might wanna put the shovel down," and then nodded to Thing Two in the passenger seat.

Thing Two held a gun on Chris.

The driver said, "We're gonna go find the June tree. We know right where it's at and we need you to help us dig it up. There's a fella back in Preston that's gonna pay us big bucks for this and you guys are comin along to tell em it's real. That is, if it's even there. If it *is* real."

Nie sensed Chris's powerlessness as he lowered the shovel.

The sun had all but left the sky and the van seemed way too dark, charging toward the gold powder harvest moon.

"We ain't got long to go," the driver said. "You two better just sit back n relax."

Nie shot Chris a look that said, "We're in deep shit."

Chris nodded, reached over and put his hand on her knee. The touch didn't comfort Nie nearly as much as she would have liked.

The van slowed down to turn right and Nie pulled the handle of the sliding door. It was locked even though the lock switch itself said it wasn't.

Damn child safety, Nie thought.

The van turned into a heavily wooded area, making it seem even darker than it actually was. Thing One pulled the van into a gravel turn-off and cut the ignition.

"You all wanna grab that shovel and pot and shit from back there?"

Nie grabbed the shovel and the empty black plastic pot. Chris grabbed the bag of soil. It was heavy and warm. Thing One and Thing Two got out of the van, came around and unlocked the door.

If the twins didn't have the gun, Nie was sure they would be able to outrun them. They were so short and plump, Thing Two looking pitiful with the trickle of blood oozing down from his mustache.

"Now, we're gonna take this here trail. You guys don't wanna try nothin, ya hear?" Thing One said.

He turned and stepped into the woods, Nie behind him, Chris behind her, Thing Two bringing up the rear.

Nie couldn't believe any of this was happening. She tried to think of something, but the red streaks of panic blazing through her head made it difficult.

She and Chris had darkness, the cover of the woods, a shovel and speed.

But the twins had the gun. Damn the gun. Could they even shoot the gun? They seemed to have some inept quality about them. She doubted their marksmanship.

They traveled in their single-file line down into a gully, crossed a moss-covered wooden bridge and started up the other side.

She decided the best thing to do would be to create chaos.

Quickly, she grabbed the shovel with both hands and let the pot drop. She raised the shovel. It was much heavier than she expected and rather than bringing it down on Thing One's head, she bashed him in the shoulder.

Her plan was to turn and run, charge through Thing Two before he could figure out what was happening and just hope Chris had enough sense to follow her as fast as possible.

The blast from the gun shot her plan to hell.

The body in the trail prevented her from running back the way they had come.

It was Chris, face down, the back of his head a glistening mass.

She froze. Stood there screaming.

"Shut her the fuck up, Vinny!" Thing One shouted from the ground.

Thing Two shifted the gun to his left hand and drove his right into her mouth, dropping her onto Chris, her hand coming down in his wound, sick and warm and wet.

Thing One was over by her side now, his hand wrapping up in her hair.

"You really fucked up, bitch," he said. "And now your boyfriend's dead."

Too afraid to scream, Nie blathered softly toward the moldy smelling earth.

"I'm sorry. I'm sorry," she said.

"You should be," Thing One said. "We do you a favor and you try n clobber me with my own damn shovel. Now if you don't give us any more hassle, we might think about letting you go after we visit Mr. Martin."

"Please. Please don't hurt me."

Thing One smacked her cheek and said, "Get up. We got work to do."

She stood up, her nervous body shaking violently.

Thing Two moved closer to her, poked the gun into her ass and said, "You scream any more and we might take it upon ourselves to satisfy certain urges. Understand?"

"Yes."

"Pick up the pot and the shovel."

She bent and picked them up.

"We need to hurry," Thing One said. "Grab the boy. We can leave the soil here until we come back," Thing One said.

"But there's blood all over it."

"Fuck that shit. Don't matter. It's Halloween. You think anybody's gonna think anything of comin up on a bag with a little blood on it?"

"Guess you're right."

"Besides, it'll be gone before anybody sees it. Gimme the gun."

Thing Two passed the gun to Thing One and grabbed Chris around the ankles.

Thing One pointed the gun at Nie and said, "You go first. Just follow this here trail up the hill. You run, I shoot. And then we'll take turns fuckin your corpse."

Nie turned and started back along the trail, traveling up the hill and into the moonlight. She cringed at the sound of Chris being dragged along the sandy trail.

The trail opened up into a large meadow. Dead autumn smells surrounded Nie, dried wild grasses and deep brown thistle crunching under their feet as they walked to the far side of the field. Darkness had brought fog and a chill with it. The fog, still settling, swirled gray and clean-looking over the ground.

"It should be just over here," Thing One said to Thing Two. Eagerly, he quickened his pace.

Maybe I'll get out of this, Nie thought. Immediately, she doubted herself. She hadn't thought things could get as bad as they had. She certainly hadn't thought the twins were murderers when she and Chris had first entered the van.

They came upon the other side of the field. More woods loomed in front of them. A storm last week had knocked most of the leaves from the trees but these woods contained a lot of eastern juniper cedars making them seem darker, thicker. Nie didn't want to go into any more woods. Even though they were still in the middle of nowhere, unseen, she found a modicum of security in the clearing.

"Ah, here she is, buddy," Thing One said.

He had stopped just at the edge of the woods. Nie stood on his right side and Thing Two moved up parallel on the other side of her, so they stood in a semi-circle looking down at... what? What was she supposed to see that she didn't?

"The June tree," Thing Two said.

"That's gotta be it," Thing One said.

The tree stood about chest high to Nie. She didn't really see anything incredibly strange about it. She supposed that, maybe, it vaguely resembled a human form. Its trunk was abnormally thick for its height. The trunk was as thick as Nie's chest. It was cruciform so it could be perceived to have a head and arms held out like a martyr.

"Why ain't it bloomed?" Thing Two asked.

"Shit, I don't know," Thing One said. "It is a full moon, ain't it? I mean, we're not like a day away from a full moon or somethin, are we?"

"No, it's full. I checked the paper, the *Old Farmer's Almanac*. I even checked online."

"Maybe it's like that old riddle. You know, 'If a tree falls and no one's around, does it still make a sound?' Maybe the June tree don't bloom unless there's somebody here to look at it."

"And maybe everyone's just full of shit. Maybe it's just a rumor."

"You think Mr. Martin would lie to us?"

"I don't know."

"You seen his pictures."

"I guess."

"Should we dig it up anyway?"

"I don't see why it would matter."

A shrill scream pierced the crisp night.

"Shit," Thing One said.

"Fuck," Thing Two said.

Nie didn't say anything.

She could only gape in amazement as the June tree bloomed.

The overall color of it seemed to lighten until it reached the color of pale skin.

"Jesus, we've gotta stop that sound," Thing One said.

The top of the tree softened, became a waterfall of dark hair spilling over the intersection of the horizontal branches.

"Take the boy's shirt off," Thing One said.

Thing Two began stripping Chris's shirt off.

Nie watched the tree as it slowly became a human female, emerging from the dirt at mid-thigh. Frantic eyes stared at Nie, shooting around in their sockets. The screaming knothole became a screaming mouth. Farther down, two rough places of bark became nipples. The tree brought her limbs down, covering her breasts and her sex, only the limbs were now arms.

Thing Two approached the tree and jammed Chris's shirt into her mouth, tying the arms of the shirt behind her head.

"All right, now take off his pants and put them over her head. Makes me nervous to look at her," Thing One said. Then he pointed the gun at Nie. "All right. You better get to diggin."

Nie put the pot down and pulled the shovel out. Again she thought about taking it across Thing One's head and remembered what they had said earlier. She had no doubt that killing her wouldn't be the only thing they did. Fucking creeps.

She put the point of the shovel in the dirt about a foot out from the base of the tree and drove it in with the bottom of her foot, suddenly glad she had opted for the Doc Martens rather than the six-inch heels.

As the shovel bit down in the soil, the tree doubled over, thrashing in pain, the pants sliding from her head. A geyser of blood shot up, spraying Nie's face.

She dropped the shovel and turned away from the tree, falling to her knees and vomiting.

"Shit," Thing One said. "We need to hurry."

Nie curled up on the ground, shivering in the cold fog.

"Fucking useless cunt," she heard Thing One say.

She couldn't bear to look at what was happening. She heard the shovel punch into the fleshy earth.

"Now we're gonna put him in her place, right?" Thing Two said.

"Yep. Take his legs off at the knee and put the stumps in the pot. She's losing a lot of blood."

Nie heard the thwakking of what had to be the shovel coming down on Chris's legs.

"Jesus, man, use your fucking knife," Thing One said.

Nie lay there and tried to concentrate on the sound the wind made as it rustled through the woods because if she didn't concentrate on that then the only thing she could hear were the muffled cries of the June tree and the squelching sound Chris's body made as they put him into the earth.

This was a far cry from Donna's Halloween party. She shouldn't have listened to Chris. She should have just walked back to town by herself. But Chris was gone now. She couldn't blame Chris.

One of the twins dusted off his hands like someone who'd just planted a garden of petunias and said, "Well, that's it. Get yer tits up here, missy. We're ready."

Nie brought herself to her feet with a faint glimmer of hope.

Maybe, now that they've got what they came for, they'll let me go.

Or maybe they're saving you for something else.

If it came to that, she would force them to use the gun.

Thing One held the pot containing the June tree, slanted haphazardly from within. When Nie looked at it, the first thing she thought of was that the tree had wilted. Her arms hung down by her sides. Her breasts appeared more pendulous. Her hair hung lank around her face.

Where the June tree had once stood, Chris was now buried to just beneath his shrunken penis. He was bent over from the waist, his face in the dirt. Nie figured he was wilted, too.

"She don't look too good," Thing One said while studying the June tree. "We need to hurry up and get that soil."

He started back along the fog-covered meadow, covered in purplish moonlight.

Thing Two held the gun in his right hand and the shovel in his left. With the gun, he gestured for Nie to follow Thing One.

Nie tried to block out the fear and any thought of escaping. She fought to clear her mind completely, free herself from the cat claws of madness scraping at the backs of her eyes.

It seemed like an eternity before they reached the blood spattered bag of soil.

Thing Two gave her the shovel to hold and he lifted the bag easily with one hand. The same bag Chris had struggled so hard to carry.

The rest of the walk seemed like an eternity.

When they reached the van, Thing One sat the pot at the rear and opened up the doors. He took the bag of soil from Thing Two and unrolled the top of it. The smell that wafted out made Nie gag. She tried her best not to vomit again, but when she saw him dump the "soil" into the pot, she lost it. At this point, it was little more than a dry heave, but it sucked her energy even further.

What came out of the bag looked like entrails and blood, all squishy and glistening. Thing One centered the June tree, positioning it upright. Thing Two handed him the shovel and he packed the offal down around the tree. Then he lifted up the pot and put it in the van, folding the bag back down on the soil and placing that next to the tree. He handed the shovel back to Thing Two and said, "Better keep that up front with you."

"Should we dose her before we get back on the road?" Thing Two said.

"I'll let you take care of that."

Thing Two grabbed her around the arm and pulled her up to the passenger door of the van. He stepped back and continued to hold the gun on Nie.

"Why don't you reach in there and open up the glove box," he said.

She opened the door, leaned over the seat and turned the faux chrome knob of the glove compartment, conscious of Thing Two's eyes burning into her ass.

"Now reach in there and grab that bag."

She felt around and pulled out a Ziploc bag, its bottom lined with blue pills.

"Pull out two of them things and pop em in yer mouth. We can't have you goin apeshit on us."

"I won't," she said quietly. "I promise."

"Why should I believe you?"

She moved closer to Thing Two and said, "If you promise you'll let me go, I'll let you fuck me."

She looked at the bulge in his red running shorts.

"I'll let your brother fuck me, too."

A sound blasted behind Nie and she saw the explosion of the gun followed by another blast.

It took her a second to figure out what had happened. The first sound was the van's horn. The fright had caused Thing Two to pull the trigger but he must have jerked too much because the bullet had missed her.

"I think you better take the pills."

She reached into the bag and plucked out two of them.

"What are these going to do to me?"

"They're gonna make you sleep. When you wake up, we'll be at Mr. Martin's and you can tell him this here tree's real."

"And then you'll let me go?"

"Just take the pills."

She put them in her mouth and dry swallowed. One of them went down and one of them stuck on the back of her tongue. She gagged.

Thing Two pressed the gun to her lips.

"Open up," he said.

She opened her mouth, the pill tickling the back of her throat. Thing Two slid the gun into her mouth, pushing the pill down into her throat. She gagged again as the pill went down and Thing Two pulled the gun out of her mouth.

"Get in the van," he said.

She climbed into the stink of the June tree's soil and Thing Two shut the door behind her before hopping into the front seat and shutting his door. Once his door was shut, she heard the automatic locks seal the doors.

That was it, Nie thought. *That was my one chance to get away.*

The van started and pulled out onto the road.

Nie sat in her seat, watching the two brothers.

Maybe I could bust out a window. Maybe if I went for their eyes. Jesus, I just want to be home. I want to be somewhere where none of this has happened. I want to wake up from this bad bad bad dream.

But even as she thought that, she felt her eyelids get heavier, her head fill up with something and she thought she could feel herself slide ever so slowly and gently out of her seat as the pill wrapped its narcotic fingers around her consciousness.

Nie didn't know how long it was before she came to.

The van was still moving, she could hear the wheels thumping on the road. She was on her stomach. Thing Two was beside her. She could smell his meaty breath. His hands were between her legs. He had slid her thong aside. His fingers played with her sex, his thumb massaging her anus.

"Man, this bitch's dry as a bone," he said.

"I told you, after we see Mr. Martin, we'll take that money down to Cincy and get us a couple whores."

"Yeah, but she's young and fresh. Her pussy's real tight."

Nie fought off the nausea and opened her eyes to slits.

The gun sat abandoned on the console between the two front seats.

The rest happened very fast.

Nie sprang.

She wrapped her hand around the gun, slipped her finger around the trigger, held the gun toward Thing One and pulled the trigger.

There was an explosion.

A spray of red.

The screech of tires.

Then she was flying.

Hitting the pavement and skidding across.

Maybe the pills were still in her body because she didn't feel any of it.

Knew she had to get away.

Thing Two was probably still alive and... and he was the one that wanted to... to... *do stuff* to her.

She brought herself to her feet. Jesus, she felt wet all over. Was that blood? Her ears rang and she was having trouble hearing anything else. She walked but her body didn't want to. She didn't hurt. She was numb. Numb all over.

The street was lined with houses but most of them were darkened, glowing Jack-o-lanterns sitting on porches for one final night of rot.

In front of her there was a brightly lighted house. Slowly, slowly, the house came toward her.

A woman who looked like Elvira opened the door.

"Goodness, honey, what's wrong with you?"

"Need to call police," Nie stammered. Christ, she wasn't going to be able to stand up much longer.

Then there was a man standing beside the woman. His hair glittered gold and he wore a pair of gold horns and, they must have been contact lenses because Nie could have sworn his eyes were orange.

"What's wrong?" the man asked the woman but Nie could barely hear him because it sounded like... *screams* were coming from the house.

"This girl..."

Such awful screams.

"She says..."

It's Halloween. It's Halloween, remember. Those are Halloween sounds you're hearing.

"That we should call the police..."

No. This isn't right. Those screams are real. There's too many of them. Too loud.

"Mr. Martin. What are we going to do, Mr. Martin?"

Nie stared at the man with the flaming orange eyes as he laughed. She wanted to run around and run back to the road but the road was too far away and her body couldn't run backward anyway so she fell forward, caught herself and tried to run in that direction.

There must be a phone.

Has to be a phone.

And those screams, high and ripe and she really knew that was where she was going because it was Halloween and she wanted to be surrounded by screams, surrounded by people.

She was through the house and out the back door, the night air, the sky spinning around her and beneath the sky, surrounding her, the screaming orchard.

She stopped, turned in circles, staring at the people trees around her, the mouths contorted as they screamed at the moon, some of them waist high, some of them towering against the sky, grown to gigantic proportions.

And beside her she felt the hot breath, heard the faint crackle of eyes burning somewhere under all the screaming.

A feverish hand stroked her cheek and, after a giddy bout of laughter, she heard the voice say, "Skin like an American beech. Don't you think?"

She willed herself to die. She wanted blood-loss or broken bones or ruptured lungs to take her away from these awful people and then she thought of Chris and wondered if it would matter.

Nie heard the woman laugh and say, "Oh, definitely, Mr. Martin."

Nie screamed. A Halloween scream. It was all she could do. From somewhere outside herself, she heard her sapling scream rise up and join the chorus of the other trees in the orchard.

Glowers Point

Karen Bruckner had just finished knotting the condom when the phone rang. She looked apologetically at Keith and took the cordless from its charger. Instinctively, she knew who the caller was and didn't really know why she resented him so much for calling. Trying to sound like she hadn't just had an orgasm, she said, "Hello?"

"Hey babe, it's me." It was Dan, his cell phone making him sound like he'd had a stroke.

"Where are you? The signal's terrible."

"That's a good question. I seem to be in the middle of Fucking Nowhere. Do you know where that's at?"

"I've been there before."

Keith ran a hand up her inner thigh and she gasped slightly.

"So what're you up to?"

"Not much, really."

"Are you alone?"

"For now. Allison and Kim are coming over in a bit. I think we're going to dinner or something."

"Okay. I was just calling to let you know I'd be home tomorrow. Oh, here's a sign. I've just entered Glowers Point, Ohio."

The Point, Karen thought, her heart leaping around in her chest, stealing the words from her mouth. Although the place name had no significance to Dan, merely hearing the name spoken aloud ripped open a dam of memories for Karen. Immediately, a sense of doom enclosed itself around her bones, robbing her of that post-coital wave of relaxation she'd been feeling.

Something bad was going to happen.

The signal got choppier. Smacks of static punctuated Dan's words.

Karen swallowed, a dry click from her throat echoing back to her.

"Be careful, dear," she said. "I'm gonna let you go. I can barely hear you." She hardly even heard her own words. She was someplace else. Closer to Dan than he realized. Someplace that had an insane logic of its own. Someplace that she never wanted to hear of again. Someplace that she certainly never wanted to visit again.

The Point, as the locals had called it.

"Okay. I love you..." There was another sound, louder than the static. Different. What came next didn't really surprise Karen. It was like something inevitable finally being fulfilled.

Dan screamed, "Oh dear fucking God!" The signal ended with a chaotic sonic jumble, followed by silence.

"Dan?" Karen said. The bad doom feeling intensified, turning into something close to physical pain. "Dan!" She knew he wasn't there.

"What's wrong, baby?" Keith asked, moving his hand up to her breasts.

Men are so fucking clueless, Karen thought, scraping his sweaty hand off.

"It's Dan. Something's wrong with Dan."

Immediately, Karen was out of bed and pulling on her clothes. She felt Keith's eyes rolling over her body.

"Aw, fuck Dan. Come back to bed."

"Shut the hell up."

Less than five minutes after Dan had called, Karen was in the car and headed for I-71 southbound, thoughts caroming violently around in her head. She was impulsive, sure, but she had no idea why she was doing exactly what she was doing and yet it seemed like the only thing she could do. Maybe it meant she really cared for Dan although, at this point, she saw it more as a responsibility. Her feelings for Dan were certainly something she hadn't been so sure of lately. She definitely didn't think about Dan when Keith was all over her, except maybe about his fumbling ineptitude. With Dan, it was clothes off, him on top for a few minutes before pulling out and coming on her stomach. If he felt really imaginative, he would aim for her breasts or, sometimes, her face. Whenever he did that, she always wanted to ask him where the camera was.

Keith wasn't like that. Today, he'd fucked her in her car in the parking garage at work and fucked her again when they got back to her apartment. But, with Keith, it was just that—fucking. Even though it had been going on for quite some time, there was no love there. No connection. And his virility had a tendency to turn brutal. She never really had to worry about sore jaws or a raw ass with Dan. Keith treated them as standard fare. With Keith, the words, "That hurts," were said in a wasted breath.

But now she wondered if there even was a Dan. She knew it sounded severe, but Glowers Point, the Point, despite all its rolling hills and full-bloomed splendor, was a very severe place.

Her thoughts ate up the road and turned the dusk to dark.

Around Columbus, the traffic thickened and she pulled off an exit. She decided she had to find a phone. Unlike Dan, she wouldn't have anything to do with a cell phone, although she wished she had one now so she could make the calls without burning time. She pulled into a BP and used her credit card to call information.

"City and state," the bland feminine voice asked.

"Glowers Point, Ohio," Karen spat. Not a religious person in the least, she had the urge to cross herself after speaking those words.

She became aware of how impatient and out of breath she was.

"That's another number. Let me get that for you."

Karen wondered if operators were aware of how monstrously slow they were. The recording gave her the number and, having no pen or paper, she chose the extra toll to be connected automatically.

"City and state?" Another bland feminine voice. This one maybe a bit more Appalachian.

"Glowers Point, Ohio."

"Go ahead."

"I need the number for the Glowers Point Police Department."

Again she chose to be connected automatically. The phone must have rang fifteen times.

"Glowers Point mergency." A uniquely twangy female voice this time.

Karen paused. What was she supposed to say? The words tangled in her mind and got stuck in her throat. The whole purpose of the call hinged upon the fact that Glowers Point wasn't the same town it used to be. That is, a town with a secret. A secret that all the townspeople knew and never talked about. She would be able to tell by the dispatcher's voice if it had changed or not. There was also the possibility that maybe Dan had had an actual emergency. Maybe he ran off the road or hit a deer or, Christ, she didn't know, suffered a fucking coronary there in his car.

"Hello?" the voice said.

"Uh, yeah, sorry. Is this the Glowers Point Police?"

"Police, Fire, and Ambellance."

Of course, Karen thought and then said, "Um, okay. I need to find out if there's been an accident."

"Ain't been none all day. Usually there is, but we ain't got no calls bout no accidents today."

No. The town hadn't changed a bit. The woman's voice made Karen think of walking into a room with your skirt tucked into the back of your hose and trying to carry on a normal conversation while the person you were talking to tried not to laugh. But there was something inside Karen that wouldn't let her drop it at that. It was futile, she knew, to try and penetrate their shell, but she pressed on anyway.

"Can't you radio someone? To make sure."

"Naw. There ain't no need fer that. If there'd been an accident, I'da hadta pers'nally call in the county."

"Okay," Karen said, trying to think of a million other questions to ask this woman. Trying to create a conspirator for her madness but, she knew, both she and the other woman were already part of the madness.

Before Karen could think of anything else, the woman said, "Okay? Bye now, honey."

Karen hung up the phone, feeling lost. The call should have made her feel relieved but it served an opposite purpose. At least, she thought, Dan's probably not dead yet.

There are some things worse than death.

No. She didn't want to think about anything like that, the creepy cult stuff. Besides, Dan's a grown man, he can take care of himself.

Karen laughed. She knew there was no taking care of yourself in the Point. Being there was half the problem.

As Karen wandered across the greasy parking lot to the store, only vaguely aware of what she was doing, the image of Jordan flashed through her memory, ripping in and gouging blood.

There are some things worse than death. There are some things worse than death. There are some things worse than death.

It was like she had to keep those words going like a chant so she didn't have to actually think about what those things were.

She sat in the car and unfolded the Ohio road map. Karen could never forget the way to Glowers Point. She had always remembered it. Although, she had always thought she was remembering it only so she could avoid it in the future. She bought the map because she thought there might be some new way to get there. Perhaps a state route had been extended or a new highway created. Hell, maybe there was even a second Glowers Point in Ohio. The last few minutes were completely gone, eclipsed by the first sixteen years of her life. She didn't remember going into the store. Didn't remember buying the map. Didn't. Remember.

What she remembered was this:

She and Allison and Jordan, Glowers Point High's most innocent threesome, had all gone down to the creek for a night of camping and drinking. After a couple hours, Jordan left the campfire to go squat in the woods. Time passed, but it was drunk time, moving way too fast. It was probably an hour before Karen or Allison wondered where Jordan was. She wasn't anywhere in the area immediately surrounding the fire. They made torches and searched a wider perimeter. Together, they scoured the trails, calling Jordan's name.

Nothing. Throats full of dread. That was it. Had the rumors finally come true for one of them?

By four AM, Allison and Karen had given up hope. "Maybe she just went home for some reason," they thought. They went back to Allison's and called the local police department and were immediately told that, no, no there wasn't anyone fitting that description—no one picked up for public drunkenness, no one murdered, no volunteer emergency calls. They called the hospital over in Dayton, too, just to make sure. The only people left were Jordan's small circle of friends.

Karen called the first one, the phone ringing. On about the fourth ring, from behind her, she heard Allison say, "Oh my God," and put her hand over her mouth. "Put down the phone, K. She found *us*."

The voice on the other end picked up. Karen heard Jennifer Gentry's mom sleepily say, "Hello," while Karen was in the act of placing the phone back in its cradle.

Karen followed Allison down the stairs and out the front door.

Through the early dawn ground fog, they saw Jordan. Only she didn't *look* anything like Jordan. Once she saw Allison and Karen, she collapsed onto the front yard. Allison and Karen went over to her, inspecting the damage without touching her.

"Call the police," Karen said.

"No!" Jordan shouted, a spray of blood coming from her mouth, ropes of it dangling from her bottom lip. Her eyes darted around in her head.

Allison, disregarding Jordan's demand, rushed into the house to make the call. Anything to take her sight off the grisly heap in the front yard.

The only thing Jordan wore was a bra, relatively mangled at this point. Blood covered her from head to toe. It was heavier in parts, like where clumps of her hair had been ripped out. As Jordan struggled to sit up, Karen noticed the series of deep red gashes down her back.

Jordan reached out to Karen and said, "He said he was going to make me like him. Something about tormenting. I think he was one of *them*."

"It's okay," Karen said, placing her hands on Jordan's shoulder.

There are some things worse than death.

Karen knew what Jordan meant by one of *them*. They were the Tormented. Karen had always figured they were as much myth as reality. Something for parents to scare little children with so they wouldn't wander off into the woods. But as Karen got older, into her teenage years, she began to see maybe a little bit of truth behind the mythic exaggerations. It didn't take her long to realize something was wrong when there seemed to be a student a week missing from the high school.

Historically, the Tormented were as old as the town itself. Call them the first rebellious teens in that area. The Tormented were a group of adolescents, between the ages of thirteen and nineteen, who broke off from the adult, church-centered society to found their own little cult. From everything Karen had heard, they'd been a peaceful lot. Their premise seemed to be that, rather than acting as slavehands on their parents' farms and being expected to follow their rules, why not work for themselves and make their own rules. Karen suspected that sex was somewhere at the center of it.

The adults claimed they were decimating the innocence of their children. They ordered the youths to stop practicing but it didn't work. Eventually, the members of the congregation decided the Tormented needed to be scared back into their senses. The adult church corralled the townspeople and stormed Black Hill, where the Tormented called home. The adults went about setting several fires, hoping the Tormented would come down from the hill and repent. Like any stubborn, rebellious teenagers, they stayed put, headed for martyrdom. The fires raged to the top of the hill but the Tormented didn't go away. Over the years, they continued to grow. And more teenagers turned up missing. After seeing Jordan that night and hearing the things she said, Karen believed every word of it.

Of course, that was only one of the legends...

It wasn't even that night in particular as much as the things that happened after.

Maybe what happened to Jordan hadn't been worse than death, but it seemed that way to Karen. As Jordan's wounds mended, her hair growing back, something inside of her seemed to be dying. Her eyes grew listless and vacant. Her skin became not just pale but nearly gray—ashen. And then, one day, she was gone. No one knew where she went but, Karen knew, *everyone* knew where she went. She was a Tormented now, no longer alive, no longer really human.

That was when Karen got really scared. She felt hunted. One of her friends was now missing from the circle. Would she be next? Whatever the Tormented were, however many good intentions they'd had, they were something different now, something akin to vampires. Vampires that, more than blood, wanted innocence and sacrifice. Karen had seen the type of kids that disappeared from the high school. It wasn't the oversexed football players and cheerleaders. It wasn't the boisterous class clown or the hoody girl who was rumored to sleep with the teachers. No. It was the shy ones. The wallflowers. The ones who went unnoticed and probably turned up at church on Sunday for lack of anything better to do. In short, it was people like Karen.

There were times she went to bed at night and swore she heard someone else's breath in the room with her. Out the window, she saw flashes of white, someone's face. She answered telephone calls with no one on the other line. Three or four of them a day.

On the night she left the Point, she woke up with one of them in her bed. She remembered him as the boy with the scar over his left eye and, amidst his pallid skin, those dancing orange eyes. She woke up because she was choking. The boy's hand crushed her windpipe and she had the panicked feeling that this was it. Images of Jordan skipped across her head, giving her an angry strength. Somehow she managed to pry the boy's hand from her neck. She had a large butcher knife in the nightstand she had started keeping there for safety. If she could just get to that. Her hand reached out. She made eye contact with the boy. His eyes were deep, the orange rimmed with black, but she didn't think they looked soulless.

"I know what you are!" she spat at him. "You took Jordan. You took Jordan! You took *Jordan*!"

Her hand clasped around the handle of the knife.

"We need you," the boy said.

Karen quickly brought the knife through the air and rammed it into the boy's side, ripping downward. He moaned and rolled off the bed. Karen kept the knife in front of her until the boy was out the window.

Karen took the keys to her parents' car and drove it until it ran out of gas. She never called back home. Tried not to think of it ever again. There were nights when she missed her family. Anger usually dismissed that feeling—how could they possibly keep her there if they knew what was going on? Sixteen and alone, she stripped in clubs until she turned eighteen. The especially seedy places didn't care how fake the ID was. Once she was eighteen, life got a little bit easier. She was able to get her GED and start college with no questions asked. Now she was almost thirty and headed back to every childhood fear she'd ever had.

She turned the radio on and up, driving the programmed route until fatigue overwhelmed her. She pulled off into a rest stop and convinced herself Dan was in no immediate danger. She convinced herself the whole situation was, maybe, just a coincidence. Crazily, exhausted, she convinced herself Dan had somehow found out about her secret childhood home, found out she wasn't from Idleville, a small town outside Richmond, Indiana, and had concocted this whole thing to show her she couldn't keep secrets from him. She convinced herself to sleep.

She woke up at dawn and stepped out of the car. After a good stretch, she went in search of the coffee machines, pushing the 'Extra Strong' button and waiting eagerly for the small paper cup to fill up.

She got back into the car, a sheen of sweat already covering her. The sweat would be with her all day, slowly oozing out. Karen cursed the car's aging air conditioner. Resting the coffee on the dash, she pulled the map onto her lap and dug in the console for a pack of Camel Lights that had been there for about six months. It was half empty. A little more than one cigarette a month wasn't too bad, she figured. She lit it with the car lighter and breathed in the stale smoke. Her muscles relaxed a little bit. Thank God for tobacco, she thought.

Studying the map, she thought maybe, in the previous night's fatigue, she had missed some other way. No. Nothing new. Nothing quicker. Frustrated, she crumpled up the map and tossed it in the passenger side floorboard.

And what if she just turned around? She almost had herself convinced she would simply run into Dan when she got back to the apartment. By that time she would be too embarrassed to tell him about her excursion. He would interrogate her. He loved to interrogate her. Sometimes she thought maybe that was the reason she was fucking Keith on the side, to see if she could still pass Dan's interrogations. If she let him beat her down mentally, then the last shreds of what they had, whatever it was, were gone. If she did find him down here and something had happened to him, she would tell him what she'd been doing and put the decision in his hands.

If you both come back.

There are some things worse than death.

But she didn't want to think about that.

There was something inside of her telling her maybe this didn't even really have anything to do with Dan. Like maybe she wasn't going down there out of any concern for him as much as the fulfillment of some sense of duty. It may have seemed self-involved but, ever since Jordan's disappearance, Karen felt like she had been chosen for something. She shuddered at the thought of what that thing might be.

Tossing her cigarette out the window, she lit up another one and forced the thoughts out of her head. The trees stormed by the window. The road thrummed beneath the car. Karen stared blankly ahead.

In a couple of hours the coffee was long empty and the highway was way behind her. She turned onto a state route and stayed with that for a while, winding and twisting for miles, the summer foliage threatening to take over the road, the bugs hitting the windshield like soupy rain. The turnoff was around here somewhere. She almost thought she'd missed it until she saw a green sign, the gray-white reflective letters reading: GLOWERS POINT 5. Almost there. Just stay on this road.

Where are you, Dan? she thought. And then, *Let's get this the hell over with.* Whatever it is.

She couldn't help but speed, the feeling in her veins a collision of excitement and dread. She reached for the pack of cigarettes and lit another one, not even remembering tossing the last one out the window. The car had reached 80 by the time she saw the yellow and black sign indicating a sharp right turn. Shit, she thought, and nearly slammed on the brakes. She managed to take the turn more gracefully than she would have thought, the finesse of her youth, the ability to take these back country woods turns half-drunk with nothing but a learner's permit in her pocket, coming back to her.

Karen pictured Dan's car going off the road. Only he said he'd passed a sign saying he was *in* Glowers Point. So it had to be after that. Immediately after that. Not that it mattered, she would be able to cover just about every road in the Point in a few hours. And then she saw the sign, hanging upside down from the two iron poles. She pulled the car over to the right.

The road she was on was the one veering up and to the right, into the hills. This was the road that could take her into town. To the left, the road forked. This road was gravel, weeds sprouting up here and there. This was the road that would take her down into the Point proper. If she followed that road, it wouldn't be long until she ran into the small trailer park by the river where she had lived out her first sixteen years. She walked over to the other side of the road, tossing her cigarette away, and stood where the asphalt became stone. She tried to figure out how many seconds it had been from the time Dan said he saw the sign for Glowers Point and the moment the signal ended. She looked for some sense of trauma amidst the shrubs and undergrowth by the side of the road. Something roughly the size of a car.

She took a deep breath. Out here, she couldn't smell anything but the woods.

Karen had come all this way and only had an inkling as to what the hell she expected to find. The car idled behind her. That was how hopeless it all felt, she hadn't even bothered shutting off the engine. She sighed deeply and put her hands on her hips. Did she even *want* to find him?

But he's *not what this is about.*

This was about her. She realized that. If something happened to Dan, then so be it. He was a grown man. If he was dead, then she would have to deal with that. If something else happened to him (*something worse than death*) then he would have to rely on some other source of help. The best thing she could do would be to get back in her car, drive back up north, and let Keith fuck her until Glowers Point was just a fading memory. She wasn't responsible for Dan. He didn't even know of her association with this place. He came in without me, she thought, let him get out without me.

Taking a final cursory survey, she turned to go back to the car.

Wait.

She saw something. Didn't she? Sure. That little blotch of white way off to her right—in the midst of all that green. Instead of heading back to the car, she took a couple steps to her right, one foot on the road, one foot on the wild grass descending down to the creek bed, getting wilder as it went.

She turned and put both feet on the grass, the woods in front of her. The wind picked up, blowing up under her shirt like a cold hand, coaxing her deeper into the woods, down into that nearly dry creek bed.

What the fuck are you doing? an inner voice screamed at her. *You're Karen Bruckner. You're twenty-eight years old. You're from Idleville, Indiana. You're not sixteen. It was all behind you. Leave it there.*

They took Jordan. They sent me screaming from my home. They took Jordan. They took Jordan and dragged her into something that was worse than death.

She found herself scrambling down the slope and stupidly thinking, *Dan wears a lot of white.*

Thunder rumbled and Karen looked up to see dense black clouds rolling over the top of the hill. The white thing moved. Did it move? Wasn't it over there just a second ago?

The thunder hollered through the hills, blowing through Karen's skull. She had forgotten the intensity of it. The rain started heavy, soaking her hair and clothes.

"Dan!" she shouted. "Dan! Are you down there?"

Not about Dan.

She couldn't see the white thing at all anymore and it was getting very dark, like going from noon to dusk in under a minute. Karen stood in the creek bed, water up to her ankles, smelling the clean ozone.

There are some things worse than death.

She saw the white thing (*worse than death*) and it looked like it was running. Without hesitation, she took off running after it, the rain and the water at her feet making her feel like she was running through a dream.

"Dan!" she called, trying to cover up what she was doing with some type of semi-rational pretense. She couldn't really admit to herself she had come back to the Point to stalk down all the nightmares of her childhood, but that was exactly what she was doing. Karen had been strong. The fear had broken her down. It had broken down all of her friends. After Jordan's disappearance, the fear became real. There is nothing horror movie about real fear. The talk of finishing up high school and running off to the same Ivy League college vanished. They were broken. They were afraid.

That feeling came back to Karen. That feeling of lying in bed every night, a butcher knife in the nightstand beside her. And most nights she would wake up, one of an eventual many, and feel that blade at her throat. Always, always the feeling of someone just outside her window, or just outside her door, or just beside the bed. Sometimes she woke up because she felt a cold hand, sometimes at her throat, sometimes on her cheek, sometimes running slowly up her inner thigh. Was that what they wanted? Her fucking *virginity*? Sorry guys, she thought, I gave that away to the first fat fuck to give me a job. And that was when she had felt the fear the most. When she had left the Point and was all alone, doing things she never would have done otherwise. Things she did solely in extremis, to stay alive another day, another week. That's when she hated that place the most. That's when she blamed the Tormented the most. When she was doing things she never would have done otherwise.

Karen struggled to the further bank of the creek, regaining her footing, and continued after the thing in white. Rain and darkness separated them. Karen's breaths became wet and ragged. A scream of thunder. A flash of lightning and everything lit up for only a second. But a second was long enough to recognize the face of the figure as it turned to look behind it.

It was Jordan.

That's impossible.

But hadn't everything else seemed impossible, too? Why, at this point, should she question anything? How *could* she question anything?

Another belt of thunder. Another flashbulb of lightning and Jordan was gone. The thing in white had vanished.

Karen kept running.

A few more yards and she came upon the place where she had lost track of Jordan. She stopped, standing there in a sort of bemused stupor. She ran a hand through her hair, holding it out from her scalp and feeling it smack wetly down on the back of her neck. To her right, from the creek, she heard a sucking sound.

Here, the creek widened in a circular pool nearly twice its usual width. Instinctively, she knew what she had to do.

That's great. Come all the way out here to drown yourself in a fucking creek.

Jordan had vanished. Karen realized part of her problem when she was sixteen was she had never really questioned where Jordan had gone to that first time. Now, here she was, faced with that dilemma again. Only, this time, she wouldn't pacify herself with answers and legends and fear. Sometimes you had to do stuff you were afraid of. She realized that now.

She looked up at the sky and wondered, for just a moment, if there was a God up there. She laughed crazily. If there was, he has to be the sickest son of a bitch in the universe, she thought. She looked at the spiraling whirlpool and, without another second's hesitation, dived in.

She half expected the water to be freezing, but it wasn't. It wasn't even the texture of water. It was somehow lighter than water, silkier. Being surrounded by it, she thought of amniotic fluid, like she was in the womb. Ridiculous, of course. Time got messed up while she was in there. It felt like it came and went within seconds but when she emerged at the end of it, on the other side, she had the feeling weeks, possibly years had passed, or reversed. Yes, that was it. She was sixteen again, or felt like it, walking slowly toward the black maw of her fear.

She opened her eyes and looked at her new surroundings. It was nighttime but Karen didn't think it seemed like real nighttime. It was like what she imagined a movie set would look like if the director called for darkness. She realized it was a full moon. The sky overhead was totally clear and starless, void of anything except the moon's alien surface, reflecting back a cold light.

The trees here were squat and without leaves and yet the air on her skin didn't feel like winter air. It was chilly, but there was an underlying balm she found comforting. Was she still in Glowers Point? Was she still even alive? There was something of an afterlife in this new landscape. Some ethereal quality. A certain level of unreality.

She captured a scent of earth, good clean dirt, rising up from the ground. There was another scent there. The smell of a smoldering fire, after the fire and smoke and coals are gone and the only thing left, like a memory, is its odor.

She should have been afraid. She had been terrified just a few moments ago, her feet on familiar ground. Now she was surrounded by something she was totally unfamiliar with and the fear had vanished. In front of her, close and looming, was what looked like a church.

The Church of the Earth, of course, she thought. The Tormented's place of worship. How was it still standing? She thought for sure she remembered hearing about how it had been burnt to the ground. Nevertheless, there it was, right in front of her, majestic in its lopsided decay.

The windows were gone. The wooden slats of the exterior were shiny burnt black and brittle-looking. The steeple truncated two-thirds of the way up. She wondered what type of symbol had adorned the top of it. Maybe it had been a cross. From everything she'd heard it didn't sound like the Tormented had developed a religion in any way similar to Christianity. The doorway was one of those enormous, arching, double-door affairs. The doors were gone, some of the heavy stones used to make the arch had fallen away as well. The whole structure seemed to somehow *lean* toward her, like the front of it was sinking into the earth. This gave the entranceway the appearance of being like the opening to a grave, leading down into the earth. She would be going in there. There was no other choice.

Slowly, she walked toward the church.

As she drew closer, she noticed the dim blue light glowing inside. There would be someone there to welcome her then. Her sense of fear was admonished by need for closure. Whatever waited for her inside, she had no doubt it was going to be some kind of ending, either the end of her or the end of Glowers Point and its ongoing pull.

Closer now, she noticed other details about the church. On either side of the doorway, hanging like porchlights, were her parents. Their hands and feet were bound. Their faces looked skyward, mouths bent and twisted. Their bodies were blackened, most of their clothes burnt away. This should have stopped her in her tracks, but it didn't. For her, her parents had died a long time ago. It had been easier to get through the day if she told herself they were dead.

She stepped into the Church of the Earth.

Is this my something worse than death? she thought, looking around her.

The hanging, charred corpses lined the inside of the church, suspended precisely at the same level like Bible pictures. On either side of her, worn stone pews rose up out of the ground. People sat, here and there, on the uncomfortable looking things. They turned their sullen faces toward her as she approached the altar. Above the altar was the pulpit. Behind the pulpit were the choir risers. These were virtually filled, the same sullen faces as out in the pews, piously turned up from their stained white robes, except these were more plentiful and mostly female. All of them looked very young to Karen.

Softly, from the risers, a voice sang out. She looked up to meet the voice and saw that it was Jordan.

"Jordan!" she called.

More voices joined in the soft chant.

To her right, she heard footsteps. She looked to see a man, a boy, emerge from a small, wasted door. It was the boy with the scar over his eye, those crazy blazing eyes honing in on her and closing the distance.

"Karen," he whispered.

"Who are you?" she asked.

"Does that really matter? This is my church. You came here. I should ask, 'Who are you?' But I know who you are."

"What do you want with me? What *did* you want with me?"

The boy laughed. "So much older and still so innocent."

"Is that what you wanted? My innocence? My virginity? You're way too late if that's what you wanted."

"Oh, I know that. The bar in Newport, where you got your first job? Remember that fat greasy man who didn't bother taking the cigar out of his mouth when he fucked you in the ass?"

Karen looked at the boy, her fear slowly returning. Staring into his face, his expression somewhat bland, she saw it shift from his own handsome face into that other face she would never forget, although the name she had long since put out of her head, and then dissolve back into the boy's original face.

The boy laughed and his face changed again, kaleidoscoping into a multitude of other faces. Some of them were men who had been nice to Karen, men she wanted. Others, a good many others, some of them forgotten, were men she had slept with just for a place to stay, maybe something to eat. Finally, it shifted into Dan's and then Keith's.

Holding out a hand, the boy braced himself on the pulpit. "My God," he said. "I think I almost made you depraved."

Karen felt as though something essential had been stolen. The fear had slowly welled throughout the boy's demonstration and now pounded along like a train at full speed.

"So if you had me all those times, why now, why here?"

The boy moved closer to her, cradled her chin in his hand. "There's more to it than just sex. You make everything too simple. In a way, this doesn't even have anything to do with you."

"I don't understand."

"I wouldn't expect you to. Here's what you need to understand: when I wanted you to come, you didn't. You had your chance to get it over with and you chose to draw it out. But the conclusion is inevitable. Can't you smell the death?"

She wanted to turn and run but the boy's grip had dropped to her neck and tightened.

"Fuck you," she said.

"When you pass through Glowers Point, you enter an agreement whether you want to or not. If you are young, then you belong to us. If you are older, then you mean nothing to us. You stand in direct opposition to us. Look around you."

Karen looked at the people hanging from the walls. Some of them were people she recognized: teachers, shopkeepers who worked in town, random faces. None of them were teenagers.

"Why does it keep happening?"

"A long time ago, there were atrocities played out here. The town had to die. The young people had to be turned away from their parents' way of life. They had to become something different. Somehow, you got away. You didn't give us time to react. But I have you here now and you're too old for the turning."

Summoning all her strength, she attempted to bolt. The boy's grip tightened, shutting off her wind, and he drove her to the floor of the church. Within seconds, two members of the congregation had risen and moved toward her and the boy. Each of them grabbed a hand. The boy moved in front of her and pulled a whiplike thing from the sleeve of his shirt. It had the diameter of a quarter and ran the length of his arm. At the end, it had a curved piece of metal, like a talon. She tried kicking but the boy held her legs down and put a foot on each ankle. He bent to raise up her shirt, exposing her tender back. With a quick gasp, he brought the whip down across her back. She shrieked out in pain, her fingernails biting into her palms. Unlike a clean cut from glass or a knife, a cut that somehow caused numbness, this cut burned with savage life. She could feel the wound hanging open, as though the very atmosphere irritated it.

The boy brought the whip down again and again. She couldn't help but scream. The fear consumed her. And it wasn't just the fear of death, it was the fear of living. In only a few minutes, the boy had told her the life she thought she had led wasn't really her life at all. She was merely a pawn. Insignificant.

The other two members of the congregation moved away. Karen realized, somewhere, in the course of this, the choir's chanting had risen in volume and intensity. The boy knelt down beside her, placed a hand just inside one of the gashes in her back. The pain disappeared.

"There are some things worse than death," the boy said, stroking the lip of the wound. "Join us," he whispered. "Join us in death."

She felt his hand probe deeper into the wound. And then another hand. She felt more and more hands on her and the chanting rolled through her head, dragging some inner part of her to some other place.

From behind her, she heard the sounds of celebration, the soft crackle of a fire. Karen realized her something worse than death was finally happening.

Cruel Women with Whiplike Smiles

Hutchens took up space in his customary seat in the back corner of the bar for quite a while before he saw the woman come in. Sitting in that particular spot allowed him to see everyone coming and going. A few moments before her entrance, Hutchens was about ready to call it a night. The smoke in the club seemed a little too thick. The alcohol had gone to his head, making him tired rather than exuberant. The house band's rendition of "Kind of Blue" seemed to drone on endlessly and the trumpeter sounded like Miles Davis if Miles had chosen to play the trumpet with his ass.

When the woman came in the door, alone, there was one of those unique pauses in everything. Even the music seemed to stop for a few seconds. All the old cliches were resurrected, ringing with a new truth. Every man watched her because they wanted to be with her. Every woman watched her because they wanted to be her. What it came down to, he supposed, was rape and envy.

She took a seat, by herself, at the far end of the bar. What life it had rushed back into the club. Hushed conversations of girlfriends chastising their boyfriends inevitably blossomed even though the women knew perfectly well why their boyfriends were staring. But Hutchens didn't have to hear any of that tonight. He didn't have to look into angry eyes, the anger only a thin coating over the jealousy—that wounded jealousy that was somehow worse than the anger. No, none of that tonight. Tonight he was alone.

He lit a cigarette and stared at the woman. She sat sideways on the barstool, her legs crossed beneath an above-the-knee jade dress. Nothing fancy. It didn't have to be. She held her drink in her left hand and watched the band intently. He found himself admiring every touch—her jet black hair pulled back and swept off her neck, her red lips, her black choker and black fingernails and the pale white skin coming out of the dress like smoke. For once, he was glad this was one of the most well-lighted clubs in town.

The band finally finished its number and the woman put her glass down to clap quietly. As she clapped, her lips drew back into what she may have thought was a smile. But there was something about the smile, something insincere and mocking, something that demonstrated how an object of true beauty can never really appreciate what is beneath it. That's when Hutchens realized he had to approach her.

These cruel women with whiplike smiles were exactly the type of women he went for. Actually, they were the only ones he could approach. There was apparently something weak and motherless about him, for these women said yes much more than he would ever have thought likely, undoubtedly realizing their sadistic control would be appreciated. And when they said no, well, it was to be expected and he didn't feel any less about himself.

Hutchens teetered toward the woman and sat rather gracelessly on the empty stool beside her. It was enough to put him in the range of her scent, which was also flawless. It was somehow very dark and clean and exotic, if that were possible.

When he turned to look at her, he noticed that she was already looking at him and he almost lost his nerve.

He wasn't a line kind of guy and all women, even cruel women with whiplike smiles, made him nervous. He said the first thing that popped into his head:

"I'm a chronic masturbator."

She didn't laugh, only smiled that enticing half-smile.

She looked at him for a long time, the way a man looks at a woman when he thinks she doesn't see him, before speaking. "I'm not much of a conversationalist either. I think we both know why you came over. Would you like to see where I live? Maybe we can do something about your problem."

Before he could answer, she noiselessly slid off the stool and headed for the front door. He followed, bathing in the scent unfurling behind her.

He followed her out into the welcome cool of the parking lot.

"Would you like to follow me?" she said.

"Sure," he said and went to get in his own car.

As he slid into his car he saw her pull around in a small black Mercedes. *All that and money, too,* he thought.

Staying as close behind her as possible, he followed her out into the countryside. She managed to go ten to twenty miles over the speed limit the entire time. Within the confines of his small Chevrolet, its lawnmower engine wheezing and groaning, he felt like she had to be having a lot easier time than he was. They sped around twists and turns, up and down small hills, out into the low, flat country where the huge plantation houses were scattered sparsely, set back off the road. With one of these illuminated, monolithic structures looming in the distance, the woman slowed down and turned onto a blacktopped driveway.

I should just drive on, he thought. *I have to be in way over my head.* Suddenly, he felt like a mouse in the hands of a sadistic cat.

A large, luminescent fountain bubbled in front of the house, the moonlight sparkling over the black water. The woman pulled her car around the arch in the driveway and he pulled in after her.

The woman got out of her car and, without acknowledging him in the least, went straight to her front door. He followed her through the cavernous, darkened house and into her kitchen. She grabbed two wineglasses and a bottle and continued with her strident pace. He almost wanted to call, "Hey, wait up!"

The word "agenda" came to mind and he started to wonder what hers was. Maybe she had found out her husband was having an affair and this was her way of making up for it. Other things crossed his mind. *Or maybe*, he thought. *Maybe she's just like you and this is all she wants. Just one night that neither party will remember too well years in the future.*

Maybe, he thought.

She led him through the house and out the back doors. Once outside they were in a huge garden, the like of which he had never seen before. Back there was another fountain, this one smaller, in the middle of the garden. There were also a number of statues—almost enough to be gaudy—arranged sporadically throughout the garden, a small underlight illuminating each one of them. There were men and women in various poses and they reminded him of the sculptures of Roman gods.

The woman split off the cobblestone walkway and, kicking off her shoes, sat down on a mat of depressed ornamental grass. She looked up at him before he sat down, her mouth twisting into that malicious little smirk and there was a look in her eyes that told him exactly what she wanted. Following her lead, he kicked off his shoes, peeled off his socks, and took a seat next to her.

"Do you drink wine?" she asked.

"Yeah. You know, I'm not real picky."

"If you were, you wouldn't have a problem with this at all. I could tell you that it was Rollin 1946, but you wouldn't know what that was, would you?"

"No. I definitely wouldn't. Stuff's a little out of my price range," he said, immediately feeling kind of dumb.

"Well, then let it be a mystery to you." She picked the bottle up and held it, her large eyes running up and down the length. "I need to go back in and get the corkscrew. I always forget the corkscrew." It sounded filthy, the way she said "corkscrew."

She stood up and moved back into the house. He picked up the bottle. It contained no label or anything hinting at its contents. *Well, this is it,* he thought. *She's brought me here to poison me.* But he couldn't see how that would benefit her at all. Then she would just have a dead body on her hands.

The woman came bouncing back out with her hands full. She sat back down across from him, childishly criss-crossing her legs. "Would you like to do the honors?" She handed him the corkscrew.

He went to work on opening the bottle.

"What's your name, by the way?" she asked.

"Oh, Elliot. Yours?"

"Magdalena."

"That's beautiful."

"That's trite. But thanks."

The cork came out with a small pop. He smelled the opening and was surprised at the sweetness of it. He had lied when he told her he would drink anything. He hated wine almost as much as he hated champagne. "This is a nice place you have here."

"Thanks. You state the obvious really well."

"Are you married?"

She laughed. "Of course. Why? Does it matter? Besides, why do you ask?"

He couldn't really give an answer. He didn't mind at all. As he approached middle age, he found married women to be the most abundant.

"Because you don't know any rich women? A woman can't have a nice house and drive a nice car if she's not married?"

"*No.* I only asked because you seem pretty..."

"Forthright?"

"Yeah, I guess. Is he coming home soon?"

"Let me give you a quick lesson about the female psyche, Elliot. Women want fucked as much as men. Maybe more, sometimes. A man could probably get off by rubbing up against a tree but it's not that easy for a woman. We ache. And the ache is way up inside and it has to be teased, coaxed, or simply beaten out. Only then do we get release. We may be a little pickier than men but the longing, believe me, is still there. The only difference is that a woman doesn't have to work to get fucked. We can..."

"Just go to a bar and sit down?"

"Exactly. Unless she's married. Then she gets to fuck when the husband wants to fuck." Again, her mouth formed that derisive smirk. "Here, hold this." She handed him one of the wineglasses and filled it full.

"Shall we toast?" he asked.

"To... to...?"

"To fucking," he said.

"And the night," she finished. They clicked glasses and quickly polished off the first round.

Magdalena was right. She wasn't much of a conversationalist. They sat in relative silence and drank a couple more glasses of wine. He found it quite agreeable. He sprawled out in the grass and looked up at the fat moon, listened to the night birds call out to each other from their separate cells of isolation, watched the slow flapping of the trees and the unmoving grandeur of those statues.

Startling him, Magdalena sprang to her feet and said, "Catch me if you can," and took off running through the garden.

Hutchens, battling with his alcohol-soaked body, struggled to his feet and trudged in the direction she had gone although he could no longer see her. Slowly, he stepped his pace up to a slow trot and jogged around the flowers and shrubs, undoubtedly trampling some of them. Once he got about halfway around the perimeter of the garden, he stopped, winded.

"Magdalena!" he called.

Some feeling other than drunkenness settled into his bones. Now he thought for sure the wine had to be spiked or poisoned or adulterated in some fashion or the other. The whole garden brightened somewhat, became somehow richer, like all the green seemed to stand out, painting itself over a black, foggy canvas.

"Magdalena!" he called again. *Shit*, he thought, *what the hell kind of game is she playing?*

After thinking that, he saw something like a path open up—a green, liquid path. It wound around a series of small yew trees and disappeared behind a huge magnolia. Now he started to feel a duel sensation. His skin and viscera felt light, his hair stood up all over his body, shivers down the spine, like it was all trying to crawl away from him. But from the middle of his body—his lower stomach spreading down to his sex—he felt a heavy thickening. This animal desire combined with a revelatory high gave him renewed zeal in seeking out Magdalena. He was going to give her what they both came here for. Relishing in the intensity surrounding him, he slowly started down the path floating through the garden like an ethereal river.

Visions ripped through his mind. He made no effort to try and force them out. The red raging fires of hell gave way to a group of sweaty, naked primitives, background drums beating as they coupled with wild ferocity. He saw a shimmering blue church and heard, from within the church and somewhere very far away, the slow chanting of "Ave Maria." A whip came down on a sublimely porcelain and feminine back, lighting a red gash. Lightning ripped through a dark sky. Waves pounded a black coast. He saw dripping, hairless vaginas and throbbing, ejaculating cocks. He could smell lilac, the mighty river, the sultry air of the Gulf and somewhere, even farther away, the scent of Magdalena.

He crept behind the magnolia and saw her there, standing still. She took off running through the dew-slicked grass, back toward the house. Determined not to lose her this time, those visions still raging through his head, those feelings still surging through his body, he chased after her.

She splashed through the fountain and threw herself down in the grass on the other side of the walk, her dress sliding back on her thighs. Hutchens landed on her, shoving that dress up above her waist and taking down his pants and underwear with one motion.

The only thing he could think about was tearing her apart. He forced her legs open and moved up inside of her moistness.

Magdalena grunted hungrily as he thrust up into her. She ripped his shirt off and bit his chest. He moved one hand under her ass and the other behind her head, moving it around to the neckline of her dress, yanking it down and kneading her breasts. Lasting only a few short minutes, he experienced everything—heard the wet grind of their skin, the soft and rhythmic rasps in her throat, felt the pumping of her blood around him. He shivered to a climax and rolled off beside her.

They lay there for a few moments, breathing heavily.

"Would you follow me anywhere?" Magdalena asked.

"Yes," he replied.

"Will you follow me inside?"

"Yes."

But maybe dreams were just starting to mix with reality because he didn't really remember saying anything at all and after they had this exchange they both still lay there. He felt too heavy to move. It felt like he was sinking into the soft mat of grass and he couldn't imagine her house, however accommodating it looked, being more comfortable than that patch of grass under that moon with that thick night air washing over his skin.

Then he watched as Magdalena stood up and sloughed off the scrap of green dress. She reached down for him from somewhere impossibly far away and he felt his hand in hers and his body slowly rising to its feet. She kept her arm behind her, leading him along. He looked at her exposed backside, the red marks from his rough hands smudged along her back and buttocks.

She led him back to their original spread. Her hands were all over him, pressing one of his arms down to his side and crossing his other arm between his chest and his stomach. Magdalena got down on her knees before him and closed her mouth around his cock. He looked down at her and she returned his stare. Her eyes were green and vibrant. Was that the first time he had noticed her eyes were green?

She took her mouth away and said, "I love to taste myself," before going back to her suckling. He felt his sex stiffen again. He looked up at the sky and then back down. She held a cup, wine remnants sloshing around the bottom, and pulled her mouth away just before he came into the liquid.

Magdalena stood up and held the cup to his mouth. "Would you like to taste yourself?" she whispered into his ear, her hot breath running down his spine.

He wanted to object, knock the cup away or something, but he couldn't move. She put the cup to his lips and tilted it up. He felt the warm liquid slide down his throat and hit his stomach and then felt like he had to be sleeping because he couldn't move and everything was black.

Slowly, the blackness of night gave way to the gray dawn. A cacophony of birds unleashed itself upon the garden. He thought he must have gone to sleep out there and tried to roll over, half-expecting to see Magdalena still sleeping beside him, but he couldn't move. He looked around the garden, verdant and dripping with life. He looked at the statues, the well-built men and women, dark gray with the night's dew. They were full of life, too, weren't they? he asked himself. A sickening dread hardened the inside of his body when he realized his fate.

Time was not a factor. For days, weeks maybe, he drifted in and out of consciousness. Every now and then Magdalena came into the garden, sometimes to sketch, sometimes just to take her morning coffee, sometimes to take a lover and drink wine, the last thing Hutchens had tasted, mingled with the last bit of life he had. Other times, she brought patrons out to the garden, told them lies about the statues. Sometimes the patrons offered her vulgar amounts of money for them. Smirking with the knowledge that she had things people wanted, Magdalena sent them away disappointed. Sometimes she would stand in front of the statues, staring up at them. It was at these times he wanted to be free, but only so he could once again feel Magdalena's skin in his hands and lose himself in that whiplike smile and those clover eyes.

The Smoke of Samuel

Decayed leaves dropping from a tree, the memories swirl back into the autumn of her mind as she sits thinking.

She slowly surveys the room. It truly is picturesque in its decay. Easels burdened with blank gray canvases surround the middle of the room like dark monks preparing for séance. Stacks of books, magazines, photos, and old drawings are limp heaps in the corners. Two stark gray filing cabinets are locked against the wall to her left. The walls are bare, absent of pictures, no life clinging to them. Dust is the only substance that clings to anything. Dirt dust, incense dust, dead cancer cigarette dust. Dust is death, she thinks, we rise and fall into dust.

After nearly a week, they had finally moved all their stuff into the sizable but dilapidating house. Samuel Bean, secretly tortured artist and alleged master of mayhem, disturbance, and vandalism at Raven Creek High School was finally settling down at the ripe old age of twenty. Married to the former Gina Blanc, aspiring dancer and general wallflower of Raven Creek High School, they made a good couple. She appealed to Samuel's quiet, artistic side, while responding well to his exuberant energy in bed.

Most of Samuel's stuff had been haphazardly sorted into the upstairs studio. His boxes of books covered the vast wooden floor, canvas-burdened easels standing erect on its surface. He left the middle of the studio open so Gina could practice her dance. Samuel enjoyed watching her. He enjoyed watching her thin, well-defined muscles rippling beneath tights or, sometimes, nothing at all. She seemed to float around the room. The silent beauty of a butterfly pleasing his eyes and sinking further into his heart.

After they had been there for a few months and were somewhat practiced about coexisting with one another, Samuel decided to sit down and begin painting again. He was mad to get back to it. The art had been eating away at him.

Once he began painting he felt somewhat out of practice. It seemed that everything he started ended up looking like something else or something that resembled excrement. Searching for a reason, he came across the only explanation he could think of.

The pain was gone.

All of his works had been driven by pain. Pain and ugliness. Gray death, black suns. There was no happiness inside of Samuel Bean.

A testament to Samuel's artistic rendering of pain was Gina's refusal when he had asked to paint her naked. "I'm sorry, Samuel. I really mean no offense. You just... well, you have a way of making things look, uh, *ugly*." She quickly reached out to catch his plummeting ego, "I'm not saying it's not good. It's brilliant, it really is. It's beautiful in its own way. But I really just don't want my feelings to be hurt."

Samuel, looking at things objectively, understood what she meant. He still argued to do it, mainly because he thought it would be a huge turn on, but she was unwavering in her stance.

Gina's observations had been something that Samuel had lived with ever since he had started showing his paintings to her. Continually, it popped up in criticisms of his work, if it was a criticism at all. Samuel had never really stopped to figure out why his art was so 'ugly.' To him, it was the only thing he knew, what he'd been raised with.

Samuel had grown up, most of his young life, in Louisville. The worst parts of Louisville. The parts that nobody ever thinks of when they think of Kentucky because pictures of the slums and the factories didn't make it into the travel brochures. There were no horses for miles and you'd have to walk through an ocean of concrete to get to the nearest mountain.

His family had moved to Raven Creek at the beginning of his freshman year. Raven Creek was a small town where everyone had pretty much the same income, but Samuel seemed to bear the stigma of living in the absolute *worst* house in it. The feeling of being the only poor person in town was coupled and tripled with the facts that he was not athletically inclined in the least and he was relatively bright.

During high school, he was the daily subject of beatings, taunting, and general disdain directed in his favor. He was once shoved into a ditch and called "nigger," even though his skin was quite pale. Samuel guessed that the fine rednecks of Raven Creek, Kay-Why, population 512, had never even *seen* a black person outside of the television, which made the KKK carvings in the school desks pretty much irrelevant.

He became involved with Gina his junior year, bringing her into his dull realm of pain. Her first taste of that, other than the rumors, was reaped when he had tied her up. Before him, nobody even knew who she was. With him, she enjoyed wide fame under such names as: poor white trash, bitch, slut, whore, freak, as well as many others that were much less pertinent to either her gender or socioeconomic status.

So, after graduation, Samuel and Gina moved as far away from picturesque little Raven Creek as they could while still remaining in the beautiful blue mountains of Kentucky.

Still traipsing in the midst of his funk and wallowing in self-pity, Samuel sat himself in front of the only window in his studio. In the mist of a gray morning, through the window, across the river behind their house, Samuel found his muse. His ugly, decaying, wasted muse. A river mill of some sort that had slowly devolved into an industrial wasteland unveiled itself in all its desolate grandeur.

Positioned between two objects of sheer beauty, the river and the lush green hills drifting steeply upward to meet the sky, the mill sat like Satan ready to be cast out of heaven. Lifeless smokestacks rose, brown brick streaked with black stains, to probe the surrounding magnificence. The mill seemed immense in its horizontal gray-brown-black structure, a line of shattered windows sitting on top of its 'X'-shaped steel supports. It looked like someone was trying to smudge it out of existence.

This is it! Samuel thought, excitedly grabbing his sketch pad that had sat beside him ever since his slump began.

He didn't know where to start. It was all so voluptuously ugly!

Once started, Samuel realized he wouldn't be able to quit until it was finished.

At first, Gina brought him coffee and ran to the discount tobacco store to get him Sampoerna clove cigarettes, happy to see him working on his ugly art again. Then her visits became less frequent, punctuated with grumbling complaints. His body, which should have been aching with unnoticed nicotine, caffeine, and general sustenance withdrawal was fueled by the painting. Eventually, Gina would only come up to practice her dance and, without speaking to him, storm out of the studio, slamming the door.

When too tired to stand up or move his arms, Samuel collapsed onto the floor, waking to the developing painting before him. A beard burst through the smooth skin of his face. New smells from various areas on his body reached his nose. He was thankful there was a toilet on the same floor.

When it was light, he could not stop staring at the vast industry, trying to capture and detail every last trace of ugliness. By no means was it a photorealist piece, but there was some nuance forever jumping out at him. Something he had to incorporate somehow. When it was dark, he couldn't stop thinking about it while he applied layer after layer of thick oils. The scenes that must have been played out there! The horrors that no doubt lurked in the minds of some of the extinct employees. The pain that seemed to surround the mill, envelop it in bleeding red. The stink of those who had, for whatever period of time, become machines or parts of the machine, fighting to keep themselves and their families alive.

Eventually, Samuel reached a point that would have been called finished if it would have been any other subject, but there was something he felt was missing. It wasn't one single thing. It was the feeling, the mood. His painting just didn't seem to encompass *everything*.

Maybe, Samuel thought, *the shading needs altered.* He covered other miscellaneous canvases with various shades of gray. He mixed every degree of black and white, trying to achieve the perfect value and failing each time.

Samuel fell to merely sitting in front of the window and staring at the damned thing. What the hell *was* it!? What could he not reach out and grasp with his mind? What, dear fucking Watson, was *missing*? What detail? What one little thing? No, it wasn't any single aspect, it was an *aura*. Not a single facet, it couldn't be given a term, it was simply something all-encompassing that would make the entire thing work. Yes, but what *was* that aura, that feel, that mood?

Finally, it hit Samuel. The *inside*. He'd never seen the inside of any factory or mill. Maybe the interior was the final veil of sadness. Maybe it was the clarity of a tear, cutting through the years of dust. Even though he wasn't painting the inside, he felt as though that would be the key. Samuel was certain, certain that all the answers to his consternation lie inside the sadness beast, the breeder of pain and death.

Maybe the workers, the people who *ran* the dead blemish were the Devil and *they* had been cast out.

Quickly, Samuel Bean formed a mental game plan. Tonight, he would rest. Tomorrow morning he would wake up and go to the mill to snoop around and get inside if he possibly could.

Samuel slept. The first night he had even resigned himself to a full night of sleep and he was plagued with a single dream—

He's almost done but he can't get off the floor. Why won't his body move? Deep blazing fire climbing the walls throwing violent light on the circle of easels shifting into hooded Druidic specters moving closer and closer to him horrible chants exiting their bodies through the dim openings in their cloaks like a bunch of dead air a song of dead air a symphony of morose sepulchral breath moving closer and closer so slow but never ceasing no hope of ceasing and the fire not spreading but becoming more alive and violent eating walls eating souls making those insane visionary easel monks more acute more pronounced as they advance and slowly pulling back their cloaks revealing what is inside so ambiguous so bright like the sun at noon on the summer solstice not even seeing everything in front of him and not even seeing What? *he screams* What is it? What!

And then the sound of being sucked through a void and thrust into that comfortably dark room.

Samuel spent the rest of the night in a very welcome, very deep, undisturbed sleep.

The next morning Samuel went into the bathroom to shave and take a shower. It felt like a great cleansing to remove his black beard, wash the grease and dust from his long dark hair, and peel back the second skin of grime that had formed over him. Pulling his hair back into a ponytail and donning some clean clothes, he went downstairs feeling fresh and new.

The morning was bright and crisp. Gina greeted him with a fresh pot of coffee and a hot breakfast of sausage and gravy and eggs in the sunwashed kitchen. The first cigarette of the day was strong.

"Good morning," Gina said, eagerly setting the table in one of Samuel's flannel button-down shirts and her simple white underwear.

"Good morning, honey. Breakfast smells great."

"Are you finished with the painting?" she asked.

"Almost, Gina baby. Almost."

He went on to explain his plans about going into the mill.

"When can I see it?"

"Soon. I promise. Soon. I don't know how long it'll take me to put the finishing touches on it but I know, I *know* it's almost there."

Gina noticed the fire dancing in his eyes. It was a fire she had not seen in a very long time. As the water and razor had cleansed his outside, she knew the fire was doing the same to his insides.

Samuel devoured the breakfast. It filled him up fast. He ate it all, regardless. After slurping down some milk to nourish his aching calcium-deprived bones, he stood up and said, "Well, I'm going to the mill."

"Wait a second and I'll come with you," Gina said, already walking toward the bedroom to fetch some pants.

"No, honey, I'd… rather go alone."

A look of hurt pride flooded her sparkling blue eyes.

"No offense. It's just, well, since I feel kind of close to the painting, I'd rather go alone. I won't be gone long. Promise. I just wanna poke around on the inside some, that's all."

"Okay. I understand." Samuel admired her deep reservation.

He quickly kissed her on the cheek and left.

Samuel stared at the padlocked garage-type door with growing anger. He picked up a couple of large rocks and hurled them at the rusty iron. There was no way he was going to get this far and then be locked out of the one thing that had become his life for nearly a month. The front of the mill dropped off into the river, making the broken windows there impossible to enter. The back of it was stuck into the mountain. Swearing under his breath, he continued to hurl stones at the unfeeling steel.

"Why won't you let me in!" he shouted and then thought, *Christ, I'm acting as if this thing were human.*

A voice shouted from behind him, "Hey!"

Samuel turned, half expecting to see a wonderful peace officer standing there with his little shiny badge in his little blue suit. Instead, it was a slight man in dirty navy-colored coveralls, supporting himself against the handle of a wide broom. "Hey," he repeated, moving closer to Samuel, his right hand swishing the broom forward while the other hand braced his back as he crept along in the gravel. "Yuh-yuh-you wuh-wuh-want in there?"

The man was very close to Samuel now. Samuel noticed that his left eye blinked rapidly open and closed while his right eye stared forward, occasionally shooting off to catch some movement in the woods beside them.

"I guess I want in there almost more than anything, right now," Samuel told the man.

"Huh-huh-who are you?" the man stuttered.

"Samuel Bean," he said, extending his hand. "And you?"

"Kuh-Kuh-Kent MMMMMMurr," he spat out, switching the broom to his left hand and holding out his right. "Huh-huh-Who suh-suh-sent you?" Both eyes were now open wide, boring into Samuel.

"Who sent me? Whaddya mean?" Samuel asked and then realized that he didn't want to wait through the man stammering out an explanation. "Well, nobody, I guess. I'm doing a painting. Just decided to come down and check it out. So, you can get me in?"

"Sure can," Kent Murr spat out and began walking outrageously slow toward the padlocked door. Samuel followed him, anxiety like lighter fluid on the flames of his anger.

After what seemed like an hour, Murr finally reached the door. He leaned his broom against the dirty brick of the outside, hunched down, and seized the lock in shaky hands. After several attempts at trying to line the key up with the slit in the lock, Samuel grabbed the tiny key ring with this one single key on it and pushed it in.

Murr began stammering as Samuel jiggled the key around until he heard a click. "Luh-luh-live uh-uh-up yonder in da da woods…"

Samuel pulled the heavy door up.

"She died in there," Murr said with no stammer. "Still in there," he added, deftly seizing the key from the lock and moving away.

When Samuel turned to watch him go, Murr was already a few yards away. "Duh-duh-don't ferget to cuh-cuh-close up," the man called from over his shoulder, raising his right hand in a wave of departure.

"Fucking nut," Samuel muttered before entering the factory.

Inside seemed impossibly cold. Inside seemed impossibly damp. Inside seemed impossibly dark and dirty. Samuel decided he preferred the outside, but his fascination and curiosity pushed him farther in.

Samuel, having felt as clean as a newborn less than an hour before, automatically felt grimy and dirty. Shattered bricks, cinders, and shredded shingling littered the floor with copious amounts of animal excrement dropped from various dwellers of the dark. Spider webs clung to every possible corner. There didn't seem to be any opening anywhere. Samuel began to feel very claustrophobic even though the inside of this manufactured manufacturing beast was huge. The darkness and filth were oppressive.

'She died in there,' Samuel mused the words of Kent Murr. *What the hell is that supposed to mean?* Who *died in here? Careful, man, you'll spook yourself out. Try not to think about it. Think of Gina. Sweet Gina.* 'She died in there. Still in there.' *What the hell!?* Who.

Samuel pulled a tiny toylike flashlight, the only thing he'd had, from his pocket and shuffled deeper into the darkness. His beam of light fell on rows of antiquated machines of mass production. They were set in rows. He marveled at the exact design of each row and how every machine in that row looked the same. They'd even aged the same way, the spiders spinning their overtly similar webs, the bats shitting the same piles of shit in the same exact spots. And he moved along the ends of these rows, not wanting to get in between the machines, afraid they may start up and devour him.

Samuel was drinking the darkness, the clotted textures, moving farther and farther back into the old factory.

Something caught his eye.

A light.

Farther back in the factory a light was on.

Samuel paused. It wasn't fear really. He had to devise a plan for he was certain about proceeding to the very place that light was on. Probably, he reasoned, it was just something the creepy Kent Murr had concocted because an old factory wasn't really abandoned if there were still lights on in it, was it? Maybe it served as some sort of makeshift hideout for a group of kids or some bums that had grown tired of riding the rails. Samuel figured he would just stick to the truth. He was a painter. He had to know what this place looked like on the inside. Kent Murr had let him in. No harm to anyone. He would just turn and walk away.

As he drew closer to the light, he had no real use for his weak flashlight. It was a fluorescent light and he saw now that it was coming from a room. What he'd seen from way back there was just the doorway. The door wasn't even open. All that light was pouring from the window of the door. Samuel could see flowers on the wall in there.

The closer he got the more clearly he could see but the scene got farther from his understanding. He'd never seen anything like it so he had to put it together piece by piece.

Okay. It had once been somebody's office but it was now devoid of any real office qualities except for the huge wooden desk in the middle of the floor. A naked body adorned the surface of the desk. Flowers were scattered all over the floor, climbing the walls, outlining the body on the desk.

Samuel opened the door, greeted with the scent of the flowers. It smelled like walking in the hills after a spring rain.

Samuel stared at the figure, a beautiful female figure. She was young and quite voluptuous in her nudity, though lifeless. He noticed her eyes; large, gray, staring into the bright fluorescent above the desk. Her skin was smooth and gray, but so beautiful, so many shades and values. Her hair was jet black, cascading in soft rolling waves over her shoulders.

"My daughter," a voice said from the darkness behind Samuel.

His heart pounded. He froze with confusion and, yes, now fear. Being in the bright room had caused him to lose whatever night vision he'd gained and the darkest of dark greeted him as he turned to face the voice. Samuel placed the voice as Kent Murr's.

Murr stepped into the bright light and Samuel realized that he was much thinner and paler than he had at first thought. From behind his back Murr pulled a bouquet of red roses that the lighting turned nearly violet. He picked up the oldest looking bouquet of flowers at the foot of the body, pulled them up to discard them on the floor, and put the new bouquet in their place.

"The prettiest things grow wild up there. In the hills."

"They're all very beautiful." Samuel made it a point to stay at least arm's length from Murr. Samuel realized that Murr no longer stuttered and his eyes were perfectly normal, sedately hooded at that. He couldn't help looking away from Murr to drink in the sight of the body on the desk.

"She's not dead," Murr said, placing a hand on her foot. "Touch her. You'll see."

Samuel reached out and touched her forearm. Although she wasn't as warm as a living human body, she wasn't completely without temperature. And her skin felt very pliant, like one of the petals on the flowers surrounding her.

"Unbelievable," Samuel whispered. "Why is she in here?"

"Oh, she was dead once. When I found her. She can't go out in the real world."

A slight moan escaped the body. A very low, sensuous moan. Her eyes blinked once.

"Sometimes she gets hungry."

Murr unbuttoned the cuff of his right coverall. The wrist was purple, mangled and scarred. With his left hand, Murr pulled a small knife from his pocket and made a very surface incision on his wrist. He let the blood drip over her lips and chin before lowering his wrist and letting her hungrily suckle. When he pulled his wrist away, her tongue snaked down over her chin, licking it clean, leaving it glistening with her saliva.

"I know what you thought, out there," he motioned toward the front of the factory. "You thought I was the village idiot. Hopefully everyone does. When Linda was alive, I was the proudest father in the world. Mr. Bean, you don't know how much I loved Linda. No, it was nothing sick. I wanted all the best for her and was able to provide it. I wish I could have done more. She always came to me with all of her problems. I listened attentively, trying to offer suggestions. Just trying to help. Then I began to fool myself when she stopped coming to me. 'She's too young to have serious problems,' I told myself. There's nothing wrong. She's just growing up. It was all lies. Still, I don't know what pulsed inside her brain. I don't know what happened to her. What led to her death."

Murr walked around behind the desk. Tears rolled silently down his cheeks.

"My daughter," he stroked her hair with his hand. "Exactly as I found her. I had to rob her grave to put her back, but she's still beautiful."

Samuel knew that Murr was trying his best to sound casual and poetic even though the tremor in his voice was threatening to throw him into incomprehensible sobs.

"I ran this place. I owned this place. She was only seventeen. I don't know why she was down here. I don't know if I really want to know. But one or more of those vile mindless beasts that sold their lives to this stinking death hole murdered her. Maybe she did ask for it. Maybe she was that kind of girl. She was never easy. But *this*. Nothing justifies this."

Awkward under standard social interactions, Samuel was entirely without words.

"I'm sorry," Murr said, breaking down. "Is this… is this what you wanted to know."

"This is, uh, more tragic than anything I could have ever imagined. I'm very sorry."

Samuel extended his hand and entwined his fingers with Murr's thin and trembling fingers over Linda's body. Not only was Samuel no longer afraid of Murr, he wanted him to feel every bit of sympathy he was able to give.

"Well," Murr began. "I suppose you got things you gotta get back to."

Samuel took his cue to leave.

"Thank you for letting me in, Mr. Murr," Samuel said and left.

Once outside, Samuel felt drained and sensuously dirty. He started home toward Gina, wanting only one thing—beautiful, seventeen-year-old, dead Linda Murr.

Gina greeted Samuel at the door, practically yanking him inside. After shutting the door, she quickly unfastened his pants and had them down to his knees. Her hands were all over him—her lips, her tongue—and nothing was happening.

Samuel's mind was back in the industry. The face of Linda Murr as she licked her father's blood from her lips. So beautiful in her death.

She *was* death.

She was darkness.

She was loneliness.

She was the muse.

And by the time Samuel started getting excited, Gina was frustrated.

"I need to finish the painting," Samuel said.

"It's been almost a month," she was nearly crying. "We haven't even been married a year and you've already stopped fucking me!"

In his studio, Samuel couldn't concentrate enough to paint. He was planning his next visit to the industry where the heart of the painting, alive in death, breathed and throbbed beneath the surface of his fingertips.

Samuel spent the next few hours smoking cigarette after cigarette, gazing between his now lifeless canvas and the dark expanse out his window, listening to Gina bang from room to room in the house, slamming every door as violently hard as possible. Eventually she burst through the door to the studio.

She stalked toward him so fast he nearly fell out of his chair. She had suitcases in her hands.

"You call this working?" She walked over to the painting. "Yeah, that's beautiful. Really fucking brilliant. I can't even tell what the fuck it is. That must mean it's really good, huh? Wait, though, it needs something." She coughed and spit onto the painting. She was crying, shaking, near hysterical with anger. "I'm going to stay with my parents for a while. Maybe you can call me when you grow a personality or a cock. Really, either one would do at this point." Then she stormed out, slamming the door hard enough to put a crack down the middle of it.

Samuel felt numb.

He spent the rest of the evening drinking beer and Jack Daniel's, winding up at the industry. This time the door wasn't locked. No flashlight now and his mind was as dark and cloudy as the inside of this place.

And he found himself at her altar, his hands running over that smooth skin, color rising in her cheeks as she pulled him to her, their lips meeting.

Linda's hands were all over him and she tasted like the sweet decay of dead roses. Samuel gasped for breath as she pulled her lips away and slid them down his neck. Samuel couldn't open his eyes. He grew weaker with each breath he took. Feverishly, he continued to move his hands over her body, feeling the heat between her legs, the hardness of her ribs, the soft heft of her breasts, and the slow, increasingly strong beat of her heart.

Sliding into darkness, Samuel heard her voice, seductive and cold—"Mmm… I could get drunk off his blood. You bring the best flowers at night, Daddy,"—and the last thing Samuel saw through the doors of light that were flying open in his mind was Gina's tear-streaked face.

Gina and her father have finished loading all of her stuff into the moving van. She sticks a stick of Samuel's opium incense between the floorboards, lighting it and one of his clove cigarettes with the same match. She looks at his painting on an easel positioned in front of the window. She's never liked his paintings but when they first met he seemed to handle her with the same passion and care as he did those horrid canvases. As she looks out the window she sees the mill sitting like a cancer on the hill. Black smoke pours from one of the hideous brown smokestacks.

'That's odd,' she thinks. She figures a homeless guy has probably found a furnace and started a fire in it.

"Gina, honey, it's all packed!" her father calls up the stairway.

"Coming, Dad!" she calls back.

Gina crushes the clove on the floor and leaves the incense burning as she crosses the room and closes the door on the smoke of Samuel.

Sad Clown, Kentucky

1.

Moments of clarity. A fleeting moment when everything makes sense. An instant when a decision is made. A life-altering decision. Charles Zasper had a moment like that. It wasn't the moment he found his mother dead. No, his moment of clarity, his epiphany, came later. But it couldn't have happened if his mother had not died. In fact, he would realize later, perhaps to relieve himself of any guilt he felt, that everything had to happen exactly the way it did for him to get where it was he was going.

2.

Charles Zasper was not an extraordinary man and the circumstances that brought him to live with his mother were not extraordinary circumstances. In the life of Charles Zasper, things just happened. And, up to a point, they happened in an ordinary fashion.

Charlie graduated from Oretown High School in southwestern Ohio with average grades. He selected an average community college to attend, planning on majoring in computer science when he finished his requirements. When he was twenty, he met an average woman, although it took him a while to realize she was average. It was also when he was twenty that he dropped out of school and went to work in one of Oretown's many factories. It wasn't a spectacularly high-paying factory, for those did exist in Oretown. It was an average factory, a paper mill that made boxes for White Castle restaurants that paid average wages and had average benefits.

Charlie and his wife, Nora, bought a house in one of Oretown's many average suburbs. There they ate, slept, fucked, argued, and talked about having kids. But Charlie had a low sperm count. Even *they* give a lackluster performance, he sometimes thought. When he was twenty-five, Charlie and Nora went through an average divorce. They had simply grown tired of one another. The good days were no longer good enough to cancel out the bad ones. Charlie quit his job at the paper mill and moved in with his mother. Between his half of the divorce settlement that came from selling the house and splitting the money in half and his mother's social security, Charlie didn't figure he'd have to work again for a long time, if he lived modestly.

Which was good, because Mother was getting on in years and Charlie didn't really have any intention of ever working again. He didn't see the point in it. It felt like he was working for somebody else. Besides, Mother needed somebody to look after her. Ever since Charlie's dad died when he was twelve, Mother had been fiercely independent. But now it was nice to have someone go to the store for her, or make out the bills, or help with some of the more laborious upkeep of the house. Charlie was that person. It was something he didn't mind doing. He loved his mother and it was nice to spend time with her before she died. It was clear she was going to die soon. At least, it was clear to her.

"The beautiful place is calling my name, Charlie," she would say. He didn't really want to hear it. He didn't want to think about her dying but he knew it was inevitable.

Charlie spent most of his time at Mother's house stoned during the day and drunk in the evening, watching television and reading books. Well, he had started out splicing his TV watching with reading but then he realized most of the books he had thought he enjoyed contained stuff he didn't really want to think about. The television was different, though. It didn't really matter what was on, Charlie watched it. Day after day, he sat frozen in front of the TV. Sometimes he laughed only to wonder, a couple of minutes later, what it was he was laughing at. Sometimes, whole days would pass and, when he went to bed at night, Charlie had no recollection of what happened that day. Well, he'd watched TV all day, of course. But what had he watched? He couldn't remember. The talking heads simply ate away his memory. So from the time he moved back in with Mother until she died was really one long continuous daze.

3.

Mother died on March 23rd. Charlie knew she was dead when he went into the kitchen and saw that the coffee hadn't been made. Mother always made the coffee at 6:30 in the morning, just like she had when Charlie's dad was alive and Charlie was rushing off to elementary school. Without fail Charlie was greeted, every morning, with the aroma of Mother's strong coffee. It was a welcome scent and the absence of it that morning stopped him cold.

Hurriedly, he went about making the coffee himself, as though it could revive the dead. He knew it was hopeless, but it was like the whole house was lopsided and insane without that scent. Once the coffee was on, maybe he could think a little bit. Maybe it would get some of those cobwebs out of his head.

While the coffee brewed, he crossed the house to Mother's bedroom. The door was slightly ajar. It was always slightly ajar when she was in it. It came from pushing the door against the frame but not hard enough to make it click shut. The slight unevenness of the old house caused the door to creep back into her room.

Mother was slightly cold to the touch. He watched her chest for any rising and falling. He checked her pulse. He held the back of his hand against her nose and mouth. Nothing. She was right, Charlie thought. She knew she was going to die. It was just a couple of nights ago she had warned Charlie about her black dreams—black cars, black curtains, black horses, and black seas. Shadow children calling from outside her window, wanting her to come out and play. And now the blackness had settled over her. It had drowned her and it wasn't going to cough her back up.

Charlie went to call the hospital and then decided not to. Maybe he should have some coffee first. Smoke some pot to calm his nerves. Pick up the house a little bit. Mother would hate anyone being in the house when it looked the way it did.

Later that evening, Charlie went to the phone again. This time he figured he'd better call the police but, picking up the phone, he couldn't do it. He was too drunk and high to handle the house being filled with cops and paramedics.

He went back into his mother's room. It felt colder than the rest of the house. Outside, the March winds rampaged, slinging icy rain against the window. Charlie pulled the quilt, something his mother had made herself, up to her chin. He sat down on the edge of the bed, put his face in his hands, and cried. For some reason, he couldn't see her as completely dead until she was in the ground. He imagined her spirit stuck in some kind of middle-ground, trying to reach her beautiful place. He hoped she could find it. He didn't want to leave her side. Not that night anyway. He went to her nightstand and rummaged until he found the only two books she ever read. One was the Bible and the other was a beat up historical romance paperback. Alternating, he read her passages from both of them. There were times when it felt awkward, reading the romance passages to his mother, but it was better than trying to think of something to say.

Some time just before dawn, Charlie got tired. He put the books on the nightstand, kissed his mother on the forehead and, pulling her door tightly shut, he went out into the living room to fall asleep in front of the television. He wouldn't open her door again for nearly a month.

4.

He woke up the next afternoon and contemplated calling someone about Mother again. Before he even got up to go to the phone, Charlie realized that an interesting sort of paranoid paralysis now crawled through his veins. If he called someone, wouldn't they know how long his mother had been dead? And wouldn't they find it peculiar he hadn't called them yesterday, as soon as he found her? Wouldn't it be considered gross abuse of a corpse or something? Christ, he didn't want to go to jail.

Eventually, Charlie settled down into a fogged routine. Every day, he tried to forget he was ignoring the fact that something had to be done about Mother. He woke up, made the coffee and took a daily trip to Hapsburg's Corner Store to buy wine and cigarettes. At first, he just bought one bottle of wine but then he found himself going for three and then four. He smoked five packs of cigarettes a day.

All day, he sat on the couch in front of the television, ripped on wine and laughing like a madman, a cigarette always burning between his fingers. The morning after he woke up with headaches and a persistent cough, wondering why he felt that way and proceeding to do the same things over. He didn't turn on any lights save the flickering glow of the TV. He didn't open any blinds. He couldn't recall eating anything. For nearly a month and it really felt much longer, it felt like the only life he knew, Charlie lived like this.

5.

It wasn't until a day in late April that Charlie had his epiphany. Actually, it was like several small epiphanies leading up to one huge revelation.

75

The day began like any other day. He woke up. He made his coffee, took the pot into the living room with him and sat in front of the television. Shortly after noon, he went to Hapsburg's. This time he just needed wine. There was still a half a carton of Lucky Strikes back at the house so he wouldn't need any more for at least a day. He jingled the door open at Hapsburg's and went along his predestined route, staring down at the tiles peeling back on the yellow water-stained floor. Charlie always wondered how it was the health department never managed to close Hapsburg's down. Charlie liked it because it was convenient, but he didn't think he would ever buy any food from there. But it was all right for wine and Charlie loaded up his arms, carrying the bottles to the front counter.

As always, old Hapsburg was there. Charlie had never figured out his first name. Charlie also realized he never made eye contact with old Hapsburg. Usually, the transaction took place with Charlie staring at his chest until the old man held out his gnarled hand to give him change. Today, however, Charlie looked up at old Hapsburg. What he saw made him stumble back a couple of steps, only far enough to where he could loop his arms out and seize the wine bottles.

It looked like Hapsburg had aged to the point of death. His once ruddy complexion was now a chalky gray. His wrinkles had become trench-like furrows cutting through that pallor. And his eyes, when Charlie met them, were a milky white. "Thank you," Hapsburg said before his eyes turned black, some type of fetid pus rolling out and onto his cheeks, diverted by the wrinkles around his mouth.

Charlie was speechless. Not bothering to reach out for the change, he pulled the bottles in close and charged out the door, his heart beating harder than it had in a long time. He didn't slow down until he was at the corner and across the street. *What the hell?* he thought.

Once across the street, he slowed down. On one hand, Charlie was terrified. On the other hand, he felt more alive than he had in years. Adrenaline sparkled through him. His skin felt hot against his clothes. His heart leaped around in his chest.

All around him it was a nice day. The electricity of spring held on. Overhead, a bruised mass of clouds floated rapidly across the sky but, here and there, he could catch the blue behind the clouds and it was magnificent.

Charlie paused at the next corner, looking around at the blooming trees and the early stages of the neighborhood's gardens. He breathed in the air, a rare fresh and clean scent for Oretown. It was only clean, he figured, because it came from some other place. He imagined the flat farmlands of Indiana. Off to his right, he saw a woman ambling from a few yards away. She pushed a baby carriage and it looked like she had on a short skirt. Charlie found himself vaguely aroused. He had forgotten how good it felt to be in that state, even if it just meant going home and jerking off over the sink.

The woman drew closer. She seemed, in fact, to be coming at a somewhat alarming rate. As she closed the distance between them, the terror Charlie felt back at Hapsburg's came back. The woman was almost right on him now and he saw that she wasn't attractive at all. She was emaciated and deathly, tight brown mummified skin wrapped around her bones. Her hair hung in dirty strands and clumps. She smelled like decay. She stopped the carriage just in front of Charlie and turned to look at him. Her eyes were black sockets. Yellow pus oozed from her blunted, truncated nose. She put up a hand to one withered breast and lasciviously rolled her green tongue out to Charlie.

Forgetting himself, he bent over the baby carriage to vomit. Inside was a stillborn, its purple body drawn up, an umbilical cord ascending to who knew where. Charlie let go with the puke, wanting only to be away, and felt the baby's sinister soft stroking of his cheek.

Charlie uprighted himself and took off running. He was only a couple of blocks from home. Ducking off into an alleyway between two shops, he pulled to a panting stop. Christ, he felt like he was dying.

Looking up at the sky, he saw the sun desperately trying to break free from those heavy clouds, lining their contours with a glaring white gold.

"What the hell are you trying to do to me!" he shouted. He didn't know if he was yelling at God or Mother or his whole sad life. "What the *fuck* am I supposed to do?!" The amazing thing was that he felt capable of doing something, anything.

He pulled a wine bottle out from his jacket. Rearing back his arm he threw it as high up in the air as he could, aiming it right at the clouds. He heard it pop on one of the roofs. Charlie imagined his blood spewing from the shattered dark green glass.

"Why don't you let the sun go, you little shits!"

He threw the second bottle. "She could burn you up if she wanted to!" Charlie threw the third and then the fourth before he took off running back toward the house, chasing down the cloud shadows racing along the asphalt.

6.

Once back at the house, Charlie realized he didn't want to go in. He thought it would be too much like walking willfully back into a coma. The inside of that house was a dense fog of twisted, half-remembered memories.

Bracing himself, he opened the door, went in, and turned on all the lights.

The place looked like a warzone. He was amazed he was able to wreak so much havoc in so short a time. Indescribable stains covered the floor, creating a sticky sheen. More stains were splashed upon the wall. A dank, heavy odor took his breath. Pizza boxes and junk food wrappers surrounded the coffee table and couch, some of them containing a decomposing mass of the original contents. The coffee table was covered in ash and cigarette stubs. A pile of empty wine bottles mounted itself against the back of the couch.

"Christ," Charlie muttered.

It was at that point he knew what he had to do. He had to get out of Oretown. To stay there was a slow death. But there were other things he had to do first. Things that would free up his mind. First, he had to stop and think—where was he going to go?

He went around behind the easy chair in the living room and grabbed his dad's old Rand McNally road atlas. It was still there. It was amazing how little certain things changed over the years. Trying not to look around him, he took the atlas out onto the cement front porch and sat down on the top step.

Age had turned the pages of the atlas yellow and crinkly. It carried a musty scent the fresh, damp air seemed to exorcise. Charlie didn't know where to look first.

He lit a cigarette and started at the beginning, reading the names of towns and cities in each state. Some of them he spoke half-aloud, rolling them around in his mouth to see how he liked the sound.

He sat there for over an hour, hardly moving, letting those names and the abstracted topography of America silence the voices screaming up from his viscera. By the time he reached the end, he had it narrowed down to two places. Going by the names alone, he figured it had to be either Nothing, Arizona, or Sad Clown, Kentucky. Practicality dictated that it would be Sad Clown, Kentucky. Charlie didn't think the car would make it all the way to Arizona and it was just his luck that it would break down in some place called Centerville or Middletown. Some generic, pre-fabricated place too much like Oretown.

Another Oretown, regardless of how far away, would still be Oretown in the end. No, Charlie had lived his entire life in Oretown, experienced life and marriage and death in Oretown. Charlie was finished with this Oretown and all the other Oretowns in the world.

His mind made up, he tossed the atlas off to one side of the porch and walked around the house to the garage. He pulled the door open and let the smell of the garage hit him—a smell he'd always found unpleasant. It was like gas and rubber and antiseptic cement with a layer of unidentifiable grime. No matter how clean it was, it always smelled that way. Charlie sidled past the car, not knowing why they even bothered putting it in a garage, and made his way to his mother's gardening tools.

Beside the table covered in flowerpots and old dried bulbs, Charlie found the items he was looking for. There was a small, motorized tiller and a shovel. He grabbed them up and went back to the house.

Before going inside, he looked around to make sure no one saw him carrying these instruments into the house. Later, when the authorities found the house abandoned, Charlie didn't want one of the neighbors to say, "Well, come to think of it, last time I seen him he was going into the house with a shovel and a tiller." That could breed suspicion and Charlie didn't figure it would take people too long to start thinking maybe he had killed his mother. That wouldn't be fair to either one of them. Charlie didn't want an exhumation to disturb his mother's resting place.

7.

Trekking through the wreck of the house, Charlie eventually reached the basement door and skillfully maneuvered both instruments down the stairs. The floor down there was a hard-packed dirt, greasy with age and a virtual lack of sunlight or organic activity. There were the narrow, rectangular windows on three sides of the house, but they were so grimed over that any sun coming through was pale and sickly.

Charlie knew he would have to use the tiller to break the initial layer and figured he could probably get down three, maybe even four feet before hitting bedrock.

It proved to be a lot more difficult than Charlie had at first suspected. Digging it took him up until nearly dawn. The old dirt had covered his sweaty skin and he felt like he wore a coat of mud. His palms were blistered and bleeding. The bottom of his right foot throbbed from coming down again and again on the metal lip of the shovel. Once he stopped, he didn't think he'd be able to raise his arms above his chest without wincing. But he wasn't tired. Not once during the whole night had he felt like going to sleep.

He stood back and surveyed his work, wondering, "Is it a grave if there's nobody in it, or is it just a hole?"

Sticking the shovel in the pile of loose dirt he'd dug up, Charlie went upstairs and out onto the porch to take a breather. He pulled a cigarette from his breast pocket and lit it, resisting the temptation to sit down on the steps. If he did that, he knew he'd stiffen up and be unable to go back to work. Because, of course, only half of his work was done. But he didn't really think of it in those terms. This next part was ritual, ceremony, something he should enjoy doing.

It was going to be another mild day. At this hour, the sun merely burned the horizon gold. Low, thick gray clouds rolled slowly overhead. Last night had been a full moon, or close to it, and Charlie felt as much surrounded by twilight as dawn. Off in the distance, a factory billowed its white steam. Muffled by the morning moisture, a train horn sounded, dragging its sad cargo along the cold rails. The world had not woke up yet and Charlie stood there, still, feeling like the possessor of some secret knowledge.

Flicking his cigarette out into the yard, he went back into the house. Still trying not to look around him, he went to his mother's room and turned the knob of her door. Bracing himself against the fetid smell, he swung it inward and then his breath got caught up in the back of his throat. His throat closed up and his heart hammered against his breastbone—

His mother, crouching in the corner, stood up, moving too rapidly, brushed the wrinkles out of her dress and came toward him. She made a hideous kissing gesture with her mouth and said, through windpipes riddled with decay, "I'm not there yet, Charlie. I ain't made it to the byootiful place." And he smelled her rose perfume covering up that fecal urine reek and closed his eyes, waiting to feel her cold cold hands on his cheeks only—

He didn't feel them at all. Pressing himself against the doorframe and trembling, Charlie opened his eyes.

There, on the bed, just as he'd left her save for looking a little more dead, lay his mother.

"Jesus," Charlie said aloud, putting a shaky hand to his chest and waiting for his heart to stop trying to explode. He thought about going into the kitchen to get some wine until he remembered he didn't have any.

Charlie crossed over to the bed and thought, "Well, I guess I have to do this." This was the part he dreaded most and he found himself questioning the reality of it. The whole thing just didn't seem like something he ever saw himself doing. It felt like he had become someone else, living some other life.

The smell of death hung around his mother. There was some familiarity in the stink. Charlie had smelled it when they went to visit his great-grandmother in the rest home. He had smelled it in hospitals. It was like the body gone bad, turning like milk or meat or fruit. There wasn't any other way to think about it.

Charlie went around the bed, undoing the four corners and tossing them toward the middle. Gathering quilt and sheet around Mother, Charlie bent down and heaved her up, slinging her over his shoulder. There was a sickening crack as his Mother met his shoulder with some stiffness before her torso went limp and draped over his back. If it weren't for having to focus on some level of physicality, that sound and that feel would have made Charlie nauseous.

Cautiously, he crept through the living room and down the stairs as they creaked beneath the added weight. Once in the basement, Charlie hurried to the hole and, as tenderly as he possibly could, turned the hole into a grave. He climbed down in the grave with her. The mounds of dirt were well over his head and he felt instantly claustrophobic. As though he was going to be buried in there with her. He figured he had managed to go a good three and a half to four feet deep with the grave.

Charlie bent down and made sure the sheet or quilt covered all areas of her body. It would seem too disrespectful to just throw the dirt right on her. He scrambled out of the hole before panic attacked him.

He stood there, looking down at her and feeling like something was missing. Mother was not the most religious of persons but Charlie felt like some type of prayer was in order only he didn't know any prayers. Suddenly, he ran upstairs and grabbed the two books out of her room. He dropped the romance in there with her and said, "In case the Beautiful Place has a restroom." Then he flipped around the Bible until he found "Psalm 23." Nervously, he read it aloud over her grave, not fully understanding it and not entirely sure he wanted to.

With that, he closed the Bible up and delicately lowered it into the grave until it rested against Mother's still heart.

"God bless you, Mom. You deserve so much better than this."

And just before he threw the first shovelful of dirt on top of her, a streak of sunlight came through one of the basement windows, impossibly bright, and shone across the dirt floor and across his mother's brightly colored quilt. Not pausing, he went about hurriedly shoveling the dirt onto her, trying to capture as much of the sunlight as possible in the dirt before the sun went away.

By noon, Charlie finished placing the last of the dirt and packing it down. The sun had long since fled the window. Charlie thought about marking Mother's grave somehow. He thought about putting her name or something like, "Here lies the sun," or, "She rests in the Beautiful Place," but it seemed too risky. He didn't want any potential owners to know someone was buried down here. He settled on a cross, two very thin lines made with the tip of the shovel, and figured that would have to do. If anybody actually happened to notice that, they'd just think it was one of those spooky religious coincidences.

Charlie breathed a long sigh of exhausted relief. He picked up his instruments and headed back out toward the garage, careful to shut the basement door behind him.

Braving the kitchen, he crossed over to the sink and, from the cabinets below it, found the jar where he had put all the money from Mother's social security checks. He cradled that in his left arm, added the half-carton of cigarettes from the top of the refrigerator, snatched the car keys from the small brass hook in the wall and started out for the car, bending on the porch to pick up the atlas.

Sunruined

1.
Sunlight

The California sunlight pouring in through the windows seemed meaningless. Paul Ward listened to the voice squawking on the other end of the phone. The voice belonged to his sister, Dorie, and it struggled to sound sympathetic but it came out all wrong because sympathy did not suit its owner. When Dorie stopped talking, Paul hung up the phone, not fully aware of everything she had said. He found a chair and sat down, his legs weak. His father had died—three months after his mother. The official diagnosis had been inoperable cancer but Paul figured it could just as well have been loneliness and sorrow. Tomorrow, he would have to catch a plane to Ohio.

He sat in the chair, sunlight all around him, his hopelessness struggling to drink it up and turn it black.

2.

Dorie

Early spring outside. Cold, but not the bitter Ohio winter cold.

After the funeral, Paul followed Dorie back to the their childhood home on Birch Street. Now they stood in the living room that nobody lived in anymore. The house was completely empty. Paul hadn't seen Dorie since his mother's funeral. Even though that was only three months ago, she looked like she had aged ten years. Always a severe tight-faced woman, her hair had gone even grayer, the circles under her intense, probing eyes were even darker.

She passed him a manila envelope. It wasn't until she used her left hand, drawing his attention to it, that he was reminded of the fact she only had three fingers. Her pinky and ring fingers were missing and she had a burn scar extending halfway up to her elbow. He couldn't remember exactly what had happened. Some kind of accident. He was only about four or five at the time. Dorie was ten years older than him.

"There is the will and the check for half of the auction earnings," she said, her voice robotic, harsh.

"You sold everything, didn't you?"

"He had been in the hospital for the last two months. The doctors knew he wouldn't be coming home. Stop pretending you would have been interested in any of it."

"It was just an observation."

"I never could figure out why you hated them so much."

"I never hated them. I just... had a separate life to live. That's all."

Outside, the rain spattered against the windows.

"Selling the house?" he asked.

"Yes. You'll get half."

Then he asked a question he had never asked before even though he had always wondered what the answer would be. He pointed to the small bedroom in the back of the house and said, "Why didn't anyone ever use that room?"

"Mother never told you?"

"She wasn't as close to me as she was to you."

"That was going to be the nursery for their first born. He never made it home from the hospital and they just left it empty as a sort of... memorial."

"Did you ever think Mom and Dad were a little bit odd?"

"I'm not getting into this with you, Paul. Let them rest. You can stop slandering them now. Have a good time in California."

And then she turned and left, heading out into the tempestuous weather.

3.

A Memory

Paul had *looked into* the room before but he couldn't remember ever *being in* the room and he only really remembered looking into it the one time.

He had been seven. Just old enough to have some really vivid, terrifying nightmares he always remembered in their entirety. After one of these nightmares, in the middle of the night, he got out of bed and went to his parents' room. They were not in their bed. He thought this was strange because they always went to bed at the same time as the children. Once they said it was bedtime then the only sound in the house came from Dorie's radio inanely spewing out Top 40 hits. Thinking about Dorie listening to that kind of stuff now made him smile a little bit on the inside—imagining something within her being soothed by all that was common and shallow.

He had wandered through the darkened house, gently calling for his parents. They were not in any room. That left only the empty room to be searched. He had no idea why the room remained empty. He hadn't really thought about it. He just kind of assumed their family didn't really need the extra space. Nevertheless, the room had always given him the creeps and he was afraid to go all the way in.

He approached the room and cracked the door.

He looked in.

He did not see his parents in the room. He could hardly see anything. The room was too bright. He didn't know why his parents would leave the lights on in an empty room all night, especially since his father, with stringent frugality, faithfully turned off *every* light in the house when they went to bed.

He closed the door and went back upstairs to his parents' bedroom, still having no idea where they were. He was a little bit frightened but not terrified because he didn't think anything that bad could ever really happen to his parents. He crawled into their bed, waiting for them, thinking of where they might be. Maybe just to a neighbor's. Maybe they were in the basement for some reason or the other. That was probably it. He hadn't checked the basement. Or maybe they had been in that awful empty room and he just hadn't seen them because it was too bright. It had to be something like that.

Paul had fallen asleep before his parents came to bed.

Upon waking he found himself in his own bed and knew it was his parents who put him there.

4.

The Empty Room

Now it was the middle of the night many years later and Paul left his hotel on Main Street, getting in his car to drive back to his parents' house and not having the slightest idea as to why he was doing this. Thick black clouds obliterated the moon and he kept the heat cranked up in his car, driving through the streets of the town and remembering why he hated his parents so much. Most people would have said it was because they had put him in rehab when he was seventeen for what they had seen as alcoholism and what he had seen as being a teenager. True, this had wiped out his last year of high school and stigmatized him beyond belief but he didn't think that was the reason he hated them. And he *did* hate them. He had lied to Dorie earlier. But he thought it was for a completely different reason than forced rehab.

He hated them because he never really felt loved. It was that simple. Maybe it was juvenile. Maybe it was self-pity. Maybe it was even untrue. But he didn't think so. His parents had always seemed preoccupied. Like there was something more immediate and more important than he and Dorie. He had always been a sensitive person. He felt things. He felt things when they were there and he felt the absence of things when they were not there.

Reaching the house, he had no problem gaining admittance—he still had the key on his keychain from his teenage years. He opened the door and walked into the empty house, the ghosts of distant years pressing down on his shoulders. He didn't bother shutting the front door all the way. He didn't think he would be there very long. He wasn't even sure exactly why he had come.

Only he was. He was sure. He was going to look in the empty room. He was going to look in there just to convince himself it was a normal room, just like every other room. And then he was going to leave. He was going to leave feeling like some grand secret had been lifted from his brain and then he was going to catch the first plane back to California and put this whole godforsaken past behind him.

It was ridiculous, he knew, but his heart quickened as he reached the door to the empty room. This was not a big deal. This was not as traumatic as losing his parents should have been but he felt a greater surge of emotion as he clutched the cool doorknob in his hand. Sure, open up the door, see the darkened empty room, erase every childhood fear he had about this room and then go back home to begin forgetting and forgiving because, really, he thought those things would have to be synonymous to him. Forgiving.

Forgetting. When all was forgotten, all would be forgiven.

He turned the knob and swung the door inward.

Light stung his eyes.

His heart hammered in his chest as he tried to discern the source of all that fantastic light.

It came from the window.

Sunlight. And now that he stood there in the room, it didn't seem that bright at all. Just odd. For sunlight to be pouring in through a window after midnight. That had to be impossible. Impossible, yes, but it felt kind of nice.

Very nice.

Exquisite.

Yes. That was how he thought of it. Exquisite. He stood there in the sunlight pouring in through the window. The same sunlight that had poured in through the same window for many many years and he saw it radiate off his skin, sneak in through his skin, lifting his mood, lightening his memories, erasing sadness.

The sunlight had meaning again. A burst of meaning, shooting through him, creating a curious revelatory sensation that made him feel like he could create or destroy anything he wanted to.

And then he was gone. No longer standing in the empty room.

5.

The Land of Laughing Children

And no longer looking at the exquisite sunlight.

The sunlight was gone entirely, replaced with illumination that was somehow more eerie. It was like the wan light afforded by an eclipse or perhaps that found on a clear night with a full moon.

He didn't know exactly what he was looking at. In front of him, towering over him, was a mansion. It was a prototypical mansion, very Italianate and symmetrical, with eight white plaster columns supporting a second story balcony. He had no desire to go into the mansion. For some reason, he knew what he would find in there. A lot of old furniture covered with sheets. Dusty mirrors that turned every image spectral.

To his left dripped a huge weeping willow tree. To his right, a gnarled live oak twisted out its branches, nearly parallel with the ground. Farther off to his left was either the ocean or a lake. Whatever it was it did not wave or even lap at the shore and it seemed to loom with its deep cobalt blue depths slightly above the ground he stood on, threatening to wash over him and consume him and everything in his surroundings at any moment.

Yet, the feeling he had felt back in the empty room remained. He felt like he walked in some kind of revelatory vision, one that he seemed entirely cognizant of at the time, like when you're having a dream and you know that you are dreaming and you do not want the dream to end. From somewhere, behind the house possibly, he heard the sound of children laughing.

A boy popped out from underneath the willow tree. Paul quickly took him in. The first thing he thought was that the boy looked Amish. His brown hair was cropped in a strange fashion and he wore heavy black clothes over a dirty white shirt. Then Paul noticed the boy's bare feet. They seemed too large and the nails were long.

"Can't catch me!" the boy said and took off running to the right of the mansion.

Paul thought he *could* catch him. He took off running after the boy, suddenly aware of the cool soft grass on his feet that were also bare.

He chased the boy around the house and came to a stop.

There were other boys there. And they all looked just like this first one. Paul started to count and stopped when he got to ten. There were more than that.

Paul's good feeling went away. He didn't know exactly why except that something just didn't seem right anymore. Something didn't seem right and it didn't seem good.

"Wanna play ball?" a boy at the front of the pack said.

"I don't think I do," Paul said, already backing away. Maybe if he could just get to the front of the mansion then he could find that beam of perfect light and go back into the empty room because even that place, that place and all of its silent, inherent scariness, was better than this place.

"I think you do," the boy said and hurled something that was not a ball at Paul's head.

The rock struck him above the right eye and consciousness swam around him, a grim nausea tickling the back of his brain.

He turned to run.

Another rock caught him in the back of his head and sent him to the ground.

The children were upon him and he kicked, trying to scoot along on the grass, trying to get away, finding it absurd that he was being beaten by a group of children. Quickly, they bound his arms and his legs with a thick rope. Then they hoisted him up and carried him.

Paul screamed.

It was the first time in his life he had ever screamed.

Looking up at the black moonless sky, he screamed and screamed, the sound of his voice feeling like the only power he had.

The boys put him down on a wooden slab. It was a table of sorts. A fire crackled somewhere beside him but the boys wouldn't let him turn his bloodied head. Instead they held it straight, so that he stared forward.

Sitting at the head of the table, looking at him with only a vague sense of familiarity, were his mother and father.

Suddenly, things made sense to him. They made sense and he put things together in his head but he couldn't blurt them out fast enough.

No. His parents had never loved him.

And he thought he knew what had taken Dorie's fingers.

Thought he knew how she had come about the burns.

And he thought he knew why she was able to love their parents and he was not.

She had understood.

She understood about the first born. About the first born being the only real child his parents had ever wanted and when that first born child had died, a part of his parents had died too because they realized something about mortality and then maybe somehow they found this place that allowed them to escape mortality and, feeling the boys' hands on his body, Paul knew they had come here again and again. Here, to this place where the first child would always live. Where he would always be born into perfection.

Again and again.

These were the children his parents had loved.

And why not? Paul thought. They would never get old. They would grow to whatever age his parents wanted them to grow to and then they would stop and they would never die. They would never hate. They would only love. Unconditionally. Regardless of what the parents wanted them to do.

Paul started to say something to his parents, sitting there with their cold eyes measuring him, but he was yanked up by the throat and carried over to the crackling fire.

Dorie had got out. Somehow, she had escaped this fate. But Dorie had always been the strong one and, as the first of the flames licked his bare feet, Paul knew he would never feel the sunlight again.

Other Grindhouse Press Titles

#008 – *Bright Black Moon: Vampires in Devil Town Book Two*
by Wayne Hixon

#007 – *Hi I'm a Social Disease: Horror Stories*
by Andersen Prunty

#006 – *A Life On Fire*
by Chris Bowsman

#005 – *The Sorrow King*
by Andersen Prunty

#004 – *The Brothers Crunk*
by William Pauley III

#003 – *The Horribles*
by Nathaniel Lambert

#002 – *Vampires in Devil Town*
by Wayne Hixon

#001 – *House of Fallen Trees*
by Gina Ranalli

#000 – *Morning is Dead*
by Andersen Prunty